Uncle Setnakt's Essential Guide
to the
Left Hand Path

To the Lady Well of the one of my oldest Teachers XEPER, Don Webb (handwritten inscription and signature)

Uncle Setnakt's

Essential Guide to
the
Left Hand Path

Don Webb

Published by
RÛNA-RAVEN PRESS
P.O. Box 557
Smithville, Texas 78957

Printed in the United States of America

Preface

Uncle Setnakt is an author who dares to tell you the truth— an increasingly rare thing in our world today. This book is an *essential* guide to the Left Hand Path— a path which leads to one who treads it to becoming more independent, permanent and perfect. These are high goals, and hence it is a difficult path. On a difficult path only those who tell you the truth are your friends. Uncle Setnakt is your friend. This book provides you with his best advice.

The history of the Left Hand path is laid out in some detail in my book *Lords of the Left-Hand Path* (Rûna-Raven, 1997). There the reader can see many examples of individuals who have in some cases become what I call a *Lord* of the Left-Hand Path. A lord is a *sovereign*— that is, one whose being is independent of the environment and whose will is potent both within that environment and within itself. A sovereign's path is self-determined, and once the sovereign has developed his or her skills, nothing can stand in the way of its realization. To become such a sovereign in one's own life is the ultimate aim of the practice of the Left-Hand Path. In many ways *Lords of the Left-Hand Path* provides a background and context which make the contents of the present book gain immeasurable depths. This book shows how our own forebears have practiced what Uncle Setnakt has taught through the ages.

For anyone who seriously undertakes the work of the Left-Hand Path — the subject of the present book — an unparalleled adventure in life awaits. No one can engage in this work and remain unchanged from the time before he or she seized on the plan. It is a plan which is generally forbidden by polite society— therefore it is difficult. It is a plan which opens the traveller up to a level of meaning which forever transforms the status quo of his former life— and hence it is dangerous.

This book is a bridge. In Don Webb's former book, *The Seven Faces of Darkness* (Rûna-Raven, 1996), he outlined a group of practical magical techniques drawn from the ancient papyri created by the Setian cult of Egypt. In ancient times many of the practitioners of such sorcery eventually went on to become philosophers who wrote such treatises as those which came to be called the *Corpus Hermeticum*. Scholars ponder *how* individuals developed from "mere sorcerers" into profound thinkers. The key to the mystery lies in the invisible bridge of teachings which effect a span between the two kinds of thought— between sorcery and philosophy. This bridge is usually made up of *oral* teachings. Uncle Setnakt's present guide is one of those rare works that does in writing what in the past was done with oral teachings. And so this book provides the practical tools necessary for travellers to design and build their own causeways, that they may become their own bridge-builders, rather than relying on others to build their bridges for them. This is the only method possible for those who would make their ways along the true Left-Hand Path.

Only rarely does a genuine Lord of the Left-Hand Path share his secrets. Don Webb, like other Rûna-Raven authors, is not merely a writer— he is a *doer*. He has spent years working along the Left-Hand Path, becoming Initiate, and then teaching real people face-to-face, designing curricula and leading a major Initiatory School. He is not just stringing words together to delight and entertain his readers — though he does that as well — he is providing you with an essential guidebook to the greatest adventure life offers.

Stephen E. Flowers
Woodharrow, 1999

Table of Contents

Uncle Setnakt Greets his Readers

To those of you who bought this book so that you would look "cool" by having it on your shelves, Uncle Setnakt thanks you from the bottom of his pocketbook.

To those of you who bought this book hoping to sincerely understand an approach to Life that integrates magic and philosophy in a quest for Sovereignty, Uncle Setnakt sends his sincere thanks, and will try to do a good job.

To those of you who bought this book thinking that you would spice up your magical life by adding a little darkness, Uncle Setnakt hopes that you will at least discover what darkness is.

To those of you who bought this book hoping to write more hate articles about the misunderstood and much-maligned Left Hand Path, Uncle Setnakt sends his regrets in that this book is accurate and will dispel myths for intelligent readers.

To those of you who had this book given to you by a friend, hoping to explain his or her practices to you, Uncle Setnakt sends his respect—because someone who has friends that care about them is worthy of respect.

To those of you who bought this book because they think it will automagically make their lives better, Uncle Setnakt sends the sad piece of news that magic is one of the hardest things a human being can learn to do, despite what the occult industry has taught you.

To those of you who bought this book hoping to ferret out magical secrets by gematria and bibliomancy, Uncle Setnakt mysteriously hints that you should buy seven copies of the book, which would be the lucky number of copies of own.

To those of you who had a rather stupid friend or acquaintance give you this book simply because you are left handed, and have no interest in the path of spiritual dissent, Uncle Setnakt sends his profound sorrow that you have such stupid friends.

To those of you who have bought this book who do not fear hard work, rigorous thought, yourselves, or the future, and are seeking the Graal in a mood of self-enlightened self-enlightening self-interest, Uncle Setnakt sends his Blessings.

How To Use This Book

This book is divided into four sections for different sorts of use. I recommend that you read the entire book through, put it away for a few weeks, and then read each section with an eye to practical action.

The first section, "The Nature and Goals of the Left Hand Path," is meant as a very basic introduction to Left Hand Path thinking in the West. It does not attempt to place LHP thinking in the context of historical and philosophical trends, save in passing reference, but rather gives a simple view of the philosophy and principles of the LHP. It is recommended that you have some background in the rudiments of philosophy and psychology, and that you discuss the ideas within with intelligent friends. This section of the book is the most important.

The second section, "Practice," is an overview of the practices both magical and mundane by which a follower of the LHP can obtain awareness and control of self and the ability to transform the world into a place of Learning, Pleasure, Initiation, and ultimately Power. These practices are no more useful than equipment in a gym if you don't make use of them on a regular basis and until you can feel the hard work of self change taking place. Just like working out, working the soul isn't convenient nor always pleasant. These practices have been designed without reference to a particular magical system— they are open-ended and pragmatic ways of changing your perception. This will be the section of the book you will reread the most. You should certainly have tried some of the practices successfully before you attempt the Grand Initiation.

The third section, "The Grand Initiation," is a Working of Initiatory Magic which will cause the self and environment of the magician undertaking it to change in four ways: she or he will be profoundly luckier; he or she will be immune to magical forces that they do not wish to interact with; other magical forces in the world will attach themselves to them; and, if they fall away from the path of Awareness, circumstances will intervene to wake them up again (rather harshly). This Working requires a good measure of self control, and is very difficult to do. It accomplishes the same magical goals as *The Sacred Magic of Abra-Melin the Mage*. Very, very few people are determined and controlled enough to do this work, which is good because it brings great power.

The fourth section, "Resources," is a brief list of books and institutional resources that can aid someone established on the Left Hand Path. It will be of greatest help during your early explorations of the LHP, but you will want to update it for yourself as you discover other useful tools. These are my recommendations, the authors of the books involved have not sought out these recommendations (and may not enjoy them).

This book is designed as a self-transformation manual for mature, intelligent adults who are mentally and emotionally stable. The change processes that a preadult needs to go through are not those which will lead you toward being a philosopher king. I would think the best age to acquire this book is about 25. Then you will have had some college, some life experience, and hopefully some travel to give you the material you need to accomplish self-transformation. This book is not scripture; it is not intended to replace your own thought and judgment; it does not make you a better person by owning it. It exists to suggest possibilities of Being; if you both partake of the capacity to be a Shaper of the Future and you have reserves of will power and discernment, this book may show you where your Throne Room is. Sadly more people will buy the book and think that they are kings, than those who will use it as one tool among many in the Royal Art of becoming more than you seem.

Chapter One

The Nature and Goals of the Left Hand Path

Sovereignty and the Stages of Initiation

The Left Hand Path is a quest for Sovereignty. It seeks four types of rulership:

- Rulership of the Inner World
- Rulership of the Outer World
- Royal Power in the Outer World
- Royal Power in the Inner World

There are two types of rulership beyond this, which are Docetic Rulership and Formatory Rulership, both of which are beyond the scope of this book.

These types of rulership may be engaged in simultaneously, but in general they are gained in the order listed above. They require hard work, mental reflection, and magical prowess to obtain, and are sought both in this life and the after life. Let us examine each of these types of rulership, and then compare the concept of Sovereignty to the Right Hand Path concept of Submission.

Rulership of the Inner World

The basis of the Left Hand Path is that humans are but machines, but may in potential become gods. The first aspect that a human has to change is their inner world. They have been taught — or rather acquired — a series of randomly assorted thoughts, notions, and behaviors most of which either actively hinder them, or at best lull them into a sleeplike state. These stultifying forces mainly group themselves into forces that oppose the body, the mind, the emotions, and the will. Each of these must be overcome.

The forces that oppose the body are those things which shorten life, remove energy, or dull the senses. Most recreational drugs, legal or illegal, fall in this category as does most fast food. Certain cultural attitudes, such as the forces that make many young women anorexic, are likewise of such a nature. The environmental factors that may surround people (from toxic wastes, to certain types of fluorescent lighting) also can weaken. The Initiate discovers these factors by life analysis and removes them from his or her life. In their place he or she will adopt a training program to make the body do what he or she wishes. The best sort of training is one that either increases self defense, such as the martial arts, or grace, such as dance.

The forces that oppose the mind are those habits of non-thinking that we have adopted believing them to be thought. We read the newspapers, watch TV, and surf the Net learning what to run through our minds in imitation of thought. The Initiate begins by limiting his media input, and by looking

3

for media which challenge his existing thinking. Thus the liberal buys a conservative newspaper, the paranormal buff looks for the *Skeptical Inquirer*, and so forth. This deliberate challenging is a first step. The second step is thought training, learning to concentrate, learning to have certain thoughts at certain times of day, and above all increasing memory. The forces that oppose the emotions are those habits of feeling generally created by external sources for economic reasons. We love to cry, laugh, or be scared at movies for which we will pay good money. Learning not to cry, laugh, or be scared at any media presentation is a beginning. The LHP Initiate has to overcome those phobias (*e.g.*, fear of flying, fear of dogs, fear of flying dogs) that hinder him or her. She or he learns to invoke certain emotional states by careful self knowledge and control of symbol systems. The average human being follows his or her emotions; for the LHP Initiate, emotions follow him or her.

The forces that oppose the will are habits of blind obedience to external symbols and signals. The LHP initiate begins his or her quest not only by rejecting sentimental attachments to cultural norms, which most non-thinking people call "good," but by actively making fun of such attachments in Symbolic ways such as a Black Mass, a Black Seder, eating beef (if raised Hindu), and so forth. This antinomian stance is no different than the stances above, but it draws the most fire from the public, because it is a reminder to the sleepers that they could awaken, and such reminders are always painful. For those of us along the LHP, we often forget how painful the light was to our eyes when we first left the cave. After the Initiate has broken with the symbol systems that teach obedience, he or she must create his or her own cosmology. It is at this point — when a unified, coherent picture of the universe begins to emerge from the four areas of body, mind, emotions, and will — that the Initiate has the first taste of **Rulership of the Inner World.**

Rulership of the Inner World means a sense of reality and purpose in what one does. We have all had those moments of power, of knowing that we are alive, and that the world is meaningful. They are rare moments and usually we attribute them to an external trigger, perhaps even a mysterious or divine source. When we discover that we can have those moments *at will*, then we have begun the lifelong task of Rulership of the Inner World. The magical name of this task is the Quest for Meaning.

Rulership of the Outer World
When we have the first task well in hand, we are ready to remanifest its results in our lives. To rule the outer world, we have to know what we like, and what we have decided is good for us. We have to decide what we are willing to give up in terms of freedom and what we must sacrifice now for gain later.

Knowing what we like is a tougher question than most people realize. Our likes have been prepackaged and sold to us for many years. We are taught to feel anxiety if our likes are different from those of our neighbors. Discovering what one likes, standing up for one's right to like it, and pursuing that desire is among the most sacred of tasks in this second phase of Initiation.

Deciding what is good for us is likewise a tough question. Simple hedonist models had a certain heyday in 1960s America, with consequent burn-out and health failures in the 1990s. The discovery of what pleasurable practices are likewise stimulating in ways to promote health, joy, and the acquisition of good memories is a personal art that must be relearned throughout life. The field of endeavor called optimal psychology, led by such thinkers as Maslow and Csikszentmihalyi, is one that all Initiates should familiarize themselves with.

Deciding what to give up in terms of freedom is a question for all humans, Initiates or not. We like the security that a job brings, that insurance provides, that having a spouse can produce. Knowing how to achieve our dreams and still be safe is more than a balancing act for the Initiate. He or she must come up with a creative solution. For example if what the Initiate really likes is County and Western Music, they get a job at a recording studio, eventually they found their own band. This transformation of Play into something that both provides material comfort and changes the outer world is the Secret that most occult books would never reveal. It is through creative synthesis of the economic realities and opportunities and a clear understanding of one's desires that this type of power can be obtained.

Knowing what we must sacrifice now for what we wish to gain later comes from an understanding of what we want, and the application of reason. If we want money and a nice house, we get a good education that may take every dime we can scrape up. If we want some understanding of the culture and art of the world, we make sure that education has a liberal dose of the liberal arts. If we want to learn to be self-sufficient, we may take a year and work our way around the world, living on hard work and wits. Choosing to do the difficult thing is made harder in that the world does not support such decisions, and our "friends" will counsel against difficult choices. Occultists in particular are bad to know, because if they have any magical skill they use it to get themselves out of bad situations— and despite their gifts, accomplish nothing. The secret of sacrifice of self to self is a magical one. Beyond the obvious rational truth that preparation and hard work pay off, there is a subtle magical truth: consciously putting yourself in difficult situations to obtain a magical Force of Being. If you really want the Force, you must do very difficult things. The simple act of doing what is hard merely to gain power over yourself creates a true Power. As it continues in your life, you will have less need of ritual, and will see more and more that things come about simply because you speak of them.

This cultivation of rational foresight plus healthy self-love gives the LHP initiate an idea of what goals to aim for. As she goes after these goals she obtains strength of purpose, which in turn will be applied to greater goals. This never-ending pursuit that pleases and informs the self by making the self ever more powerful in the world is called the Acquisition of Strength.

5

Royal Power in the Outer World

Human beings have two desires that lead them to their third task, the making of other human beings better. The first is a weak and vain desire that RHP creeds strike out against, which is the desire to show off. The second is a desire that generally makes us good herd animals, the desire to help out other people. This second desire is generally derided by the more immature forms of the Left Hand Path. By understanding and accepting these desires, we can not only engage in the pleasures that come from them, but also transform ourselves into yet more Sovereign beings.

The desire to show off is generally used by forces outside of ourselves for their gain. They sell us a snazzy car, a bigger computer, or nicer clothes than our neighbors'. Good primates that we are, we fall for this trick every time (yet more proof that man is machine). But we can use this desire to our advantage by learning to show off displays of wisdom and virtue, which will attract a certain type of individual. This is a good first step in that it takes rulership of the desire away from an external force, and places it with an internal one. But it leads to the guru game— a large pool of followers that admire us, while we bask in a wisdom that is small. So if we decide that we will make ourselves wiser and more powerful so that we will have more to Teach, we can indulge in the follower game all our lives. However this leads to a second dilemma. As we get better, we also have to help others get better so that we have people to talk to, and they in turn begin to desire followers (having the same weakness and vanity that we do). Slowly we change our desire to show off into a desire for peers, and thus we create schools that perpetuate our thoughts.

The desire to help out people comes from the refinement of the emotions. Most people begin the Left Hand Path in a state of disillusionment and rebellion. They want to be boss rather then be bossed. (In fact everyone is on the LHP for two weeks when they are 17.) The emotional states here are anger and greed and jealousy. This dark side of human nature is where the Good will come from (the Shadow is the Initiator), but as self-power is gained, so comes the capacity for a non-sentimental love of others. The LHP Initiate, recognizing as virtues personal strength and self knowledge, does what he or she can to help others create the states. If this emotion is not carefully watched, it can devolve into a dangerous sentimentality that causes us to make things too easy on those who come after us, but if it is carefully refined in the light of one's own past experiences, it can become an igniting force— a spark that awakens the Gifted but sleeping members of mankind.

If these two desires are carefully blended, balanced, and brought to bear with the hard-won wisdom of the first two tasks, the Initiate has a great magnetic power. He or she can take the circumstances of others around him or her and turn them into an endless process of refinement. He can help his students get over the death of a friend, she can help her employees cope with changing working conditions, and so forth. Everything that happens around them becomes an opportunity for those who would be better to get better. While this great benefit is being visited upon others, the Initiate, in merely considering what to do or say to his friends,

6

followers, or fellow travelers, is refining his or her own thoughts and moods. By initiating others, self initiation is furthered— both by articulation and seeing whether or not one's theories work in the world. The magical name for this state is the Practice of Alchemy.

Royal Power in the Inner World

Consider what sort of things have been obtained by this point. By now Initiates have gained control of their environments. They can place themselves in such situations as lead to a productive ordering of their inner world (they have learned how to Learn). They can choose those activities in the world that cause their inborn talents and strengths to flourish (they have learned how to Grow). They have learned how to Teach others the first two steps by word **and** example (they have learned how to Initiate). Now they can take on the inner darkness and make it glow with its own self-created light.

Human beings are besieged with four self-fears. After they have met their outward-directed fears (fear of want, fear of violence, fear of abandonment, and so forth), the inward-directed fears remain. Among the inward-directed fears are:

1. Fear of the unknown impulse (or the Imp of the Perverse),
2. Fear of the future,
3. Fear of wasted time, and
4. Fear of the unverifiable.

Each of these fears stops action, sours life, and limits one's sovereignty. Let us identify each in turn, and explain how the fourth phase of Initiation gives opportunity to overcome these fears.

Fear of the unknown impulse. How many times has your life taken a certain turn, based on no clear reason? You decided to go into a store on an impulse, and met your spouse. You decided to pick up a slip of paper off the floor, and found your college major. You disagreed with a family member over the Thanksgiving day menu, and wound up with a fight that scarred you both for life.

The Left Hand Path magician comes to realize that such "slips" and seeming "accidents" are the key to power. But this does not mean that he or she believes that every event is fated. It means that learning to control one's life rationally becomes a talisman to effect control of the Hidden aspects of life as well. Thus magicians will enter a phase where none of their actions are random or accidental, and learn to watch themselves as a great source of Mystery, from which even more being can be gained.

Fear of the future. We are compelled to act, but not know the consequences of our actions. As humans we deal with this with a form of auto-hypnosis called cognitive dissonance. We learn to justify our choices. So each movement towards freedom actually becomes a movement toward binding one's life on the outer-directed notion of one's history. Given the abilities that have been obtained by this stage of being, the Initiate can now actually abandon cognitive dissonance and take full responsibility for the future by admitting that it is unknown— it is the Great Darkness out of which all things are manifested. The Initiate armed with their inner strengths can learn to act in such a manner that will make them feel good about their choices. This simple-sounding state is one of the most difficult to accomplish, but when it comes a certain power — a certain confidence — flows from the Initiate that causes all around them to follow him or her.

Fear of wasted time. By the time in our lives that we have reached the fourth phase of Initiation, we are already experiencing the dimming of youth. We have begun to hear Death's snigger rather plainly, and we are apt to be caught in the fear of wasted time. Do I spend my time learning the Runes, starting a new business, solving my family dilemmas? The experiences of the three types of Sovereignty gained so far must be used now to Learn the life lesson, that if you continue to act with an Initiatory attitude all life experiences can be used in the Quest for Sovereignty. The choice is not finding *the* right thing to do, but finding the right attitude that informs your actions.

Fear of the unverifiable. All humans on any religious or philosophical path fear that in the end there is no "proof" of what is believed. The Quest for Immortality might be a unicorn-hunt, the Quest for Sovereignty might be just good psychology for motivating ourselves for years. But this fourth stage of the Quest for Sovereignty gives us the test of our ideas. As we begin to unlock the darkness within, our "accidents" and "slips" begin to take us to places where the Truths of our lives can be uncovered. As we exude confidence we attract the type of Seeker that wants to put forth what we have, so we have a living laboratory to see if our ideas work. As we discover the nature of attitude, we begin to Understand what has gone on in our lives, and who we are— we forgive ourselves for wasted time, and learn how to make the remaining decades of our lives powerful and joyous. These states give us the proof of our subjective state. Unlike a Right Hand Path prophet who must imagine that he hears a voice in a burning bush, we hear our own voice explaining our lives to us.

Throughout mankind's history, certain men and women have obtained to this fourth level of Initiation. They have been, are, and will be, the true Black Order, who by their Strivings bring new impulses to the Earth while living and beyond, and thus effect the Work of the Prince of Darkness in creating the historical conditions needed for certain qualities to come to exist in mankind such as bravery, curiosity, love, and contemplation. This Order has many outward names, but only one Essence.

These four phases of the Quest for Sovereignty have two things in common. Firstly they are not entirely linear, and secondly we always believe that we have obtained and mastered them years before we do so. The first leads to great discoveries early in the magical career, and is a blessed thing. The second leads to laziness and arrogance, and is accursed by all true philosophers.

The Nature of the Self and the Cosmos

The practice of initiation is discovering the essential and interacting with it. We have a linguistic model of what the essential is. It is how and why we create nouns and verbs. We don't for example have a name for every single cow ("You're Bossy, and you're Maribell, and I've got 40,000 more in the herd to name today.") We have one word that points to the essence of the experience of cowness, that is to say, "cow." The essential aspects of life— whether in our inner world, the microcosm, the Self; or in the outer world, the Other— must be identified, understood, and interacted with. This interaction is done for the purpose of self development, and may require us to act on the Essence, the Essence to act on us, or a mutual interaction.

To identify these essences the levels at which they are manifest must be known, and the rules with which they can be interacted with must be discovered.

To change the Self, you must first know what the Self is, and where pressures can be applied to achieve change. The magical self consists of four levels of dynamism, each with its own properties. They are the surface level, the medial level, the core level, and the daemonic level.

The *surface level* is the activities in the here-and-now. The changes wrought here are the most important to the development of the Self on Earth, yet for the most part they are of no consequence. A wrong turn of the wheel of your car may end your life, but deciding whether to have a cup of coffee is not likely to have that much impact in ten years. The magician has one way of effecting this level of activity. It is the formula of Awaken, See, Act. The first part of the formula **Awaken** assumes two things. One, that I have fallen asleep (and need to refocus my mind/body/soul). Two, that since the Subjective Universe has no location in time and space— any moment and any place can be a launching pad both to and from it. **See** assumes that I don't really know what is going on, and that surface appearances are misleading (*i.e.*, the smiling man from the insurance company isn't really interested in my well being). The third term **Act** means that I must, in my quest for Sovereignty, Do something. The Symbol of the surface level of being is the Enneagram. The surface level of being provides Freedom.

The *medial level* is the area most subject to programming. It is the part of the self where goals, dreams, habits, and desires lay. The human being is constantly full of notions, usually unexamined, about what he or she would like to do and "should" do. Sometimes these notions are in conflict, often they are based on delusion. This area has to be cleared of unwanted programming, and filled with wanted programming. This part of the self is most easily effected by two forces: Self-Knowledge and Magic. Knowledge is an understanding of happiness and limits. Happiness is a self-determined and self-perceived state. Not only is what makes me happy not what makes you happy, it is very likely that you have seldom known magical happiness, because you do not know your character. Magical happiness is not mere gratification, it is that which engages the greatest parts of your being. It is not the result of Indulgence, which is the state

9

granted by those things with which we can temporarily gain union; magical happiness is the state of *knowing who you are by what has made you happy.* Knowledge is based on a true understanding of limits of self. You won't be playing for the NBA if you are five foot two. You won't be Miss America if you're missing your two front teeth. Knowing your limits, knowing exactly what you are and then using your assets and overcoming your shortcomings, is the key to happiness. Magic is the art of changing one's medial activity so that certain results may be obtained in the inner and outer worlds. Magic can be useful in breaking bad habits, obtaining new perceptions, obtaining new resources and opportunities in the world; but its main use is in changing Perception. Magic allows you to see the world more and more from the point of view of a constant to which all else becomes a variable. This part of our existence is seldom perceived since our attention is usually within it. Unchecked, it is a place of worry and despair or idle daydreaming. When all of our attention is lost in the medial level, things feel unreal to us, or our friends tell us (quite correctly) that we are in denial. When we have balanced the medial level of ourselves, the symbols of our dreams are coherent. The medial level of activity can be directly observed as the "near-death experience." Many people, myself among them, have had the interesting feature of their "life passing before their eyes" in a near-death experience. This rapid, deep, and surprising experience shows the value many events have had on shaping you. It clarifies many things. It also shows things that not only you would rather forget, but that indeed you had forgotten. Most people confronted by this kind of death experience will suffer at having done so little. "Gee, you mean at any time I could have done something about my wretched little life? Why didn't someone tell me?" The Symbol of the medial level of being is the Jungian mandala. The medial level of being provides Context.

The *core level* of dynamism is the unchangeable part of the Self. It exists as an absolute pattern for potential. In many myths, the core part of ourselves is the first land, the magical island rising from the watery depths. Here is that part of you which is unique, indestructible, and not directly observable— but its presence in the Cosmos sets up those situations that cause you to become aware firstly of your own existence, and then to sense what sorts of experiences might help with your development. It is, in short, the reason for your unique existence, and all furthering of its development is the Work of the Left Hand Path. It is rarely perceived in our lives since our attention is loosely housed there. The core level of being is not static since it contains the principle of dynamism. The name for this core level is the Principle of Isolate Intelligence. The Symbol for the core level of being is the Inverse Pentagram surrounded by a circle. The core level of being provides Individuality.

The *daemonic level* of activity is that experience that associated you with what are vaguely called "magical currents." This part of ourselves, which is as ununified and semi-sleeping as the others, is the part of ourselves that acts upon the Cosmos, and is acted upon by entities in the

Cosmos on a magical level. It has access to data that is not bound in chronological time, it can cause effects at a distance, it can lead you to items and persons that are desirable even if you do not recognize their qualities due to their surface manifestations. It can even be seen under certain circumstances. This level of being may be partially inherited such as the Germanic *fylgja* or the Celtic banshee, or it may be invoked like the Holy Guardian Angel. The Symbol for this part of being is a Mirror. The daemonic level of being provides Magic.

Each of these parts must be awakened, its subcomponents harmonized, its place in the personal ecology controlled and regulated. Each of these parts is fed by and feeds the other parts.

The Cosmos has exactly the same four levels. By changing the four levels of yourself, the Microcosm, the Cosmos may be effected by Resonance. By studying the four levels of yourself, you may learn about the four levels of the Cosmos, and by studying the levels of the Cosmos you may learn about yourself. Let us look briefly at the four levels of the Cosmos.

The surface level. Here the Cosmos is very small: it is only that section that is interacting with you at a given moment. Even so, it is larger than you, and will remain largely hidden in the ways it is affecting you. A guideline for understanding this level of the Cosmos is that it is the exercise equipment, you are the gym customer. There is nothing that is coming your way in a given moment that you are not strong enough to handle. The surface level provides Energy. Its Symbol is a Triangle whose angles touch a circle; this is a reminder of the Cycles of coming into being, exerting constant force, and passing away from being that bind all aspects of the perceivable world.

The medial level. This is the sum total of all the subjective overlays that determine human events. This means what some occultists call the "World Soul," historians are apt are to call the "zeitgeist," and what futurists call "trends." The medial level is composed of historical forces, semiconscious remnants of thought systems, advertising, and herd prejudices. The forces in this heady mix are always in conflict. All of these forces act to take the place of thinking in individual human beings by a form of hypnosis. If the magician can learn to avoid the "spell" these forces place upon him or her, they are then free to use these forces. The magician realizes that these forces are Neutral in his or her struggle— that means that at any given moment about half of the forces are against you, and half on your side. The medial level of the Cosmos provides the magician with his or her unawakened Allies for various political, artistic, and social endeavors. The Symbol for the medial level of the world is an eight-rayed circle, which is identified with the Chaos Magic movement.

The core level. The Left Hand Path posits that its patron the Prince of Darkness, the ultimate source of patterns and potentialities, is the core level of the Cosmos. The Prince of Darkness *chooses* to be a finite being, so that It may enjoy its individuality. Unlike the all-powerful, all-encompassing being that the Right Hand Path would envision as God, the Prince of Darkness chose, on a Cosmic level what those who would grow like him choose on a human level— the principle of Self-development. The core level of the Cosmos provides the Model of divine individuality and independence. The Symbol for the Prince of Darkness is culturally determined. In a society ruled by Right Hand Path paradigms, the Prince of Darkness is the rebel against cosmic injustice, Satan. In a society where the release of energy from dissipating patterns is revered yet feared, it is Shiva. In a society that stresses the role of the LHP magician as culture hero, it will be the supreme god of the pantheon like Odhinn or Tezcatlipoca. In a society where there is no central paradigm but many competing at the same time, it will be Set, the god against the gods.

The daemonic level. This is the sum total of all magical activity in the world. The spells and enchantments that have Shaped the world are still active in it. Some are fairly obvious: The interactions of Dr. John Dee with Elizabeth I are why English is the primary language in the United Sates and Canada. Others are a tad more obscure, such as the hippie culture's roots in Aleister Crowley's introducing Huxley to mescaline. Some may be of very small scale, such as a haunting, or as vast and mysterious as megaliths. These forces tend to prey on most would-be magicians causing them to "bow down" to the achievements of a past they are not wise enough to understand. But for those who see such things as triumphs of the human spirit, and use them as spurs to their own greatness, these magics of the past provide aid both as inspiration and amplification. The Left Hand Path initiate studies manifestations in the following manner.

1. They begin with research in current scholarly resources on matters of interest. The Left Hand Path magician avoids the occultnik drek that reflects another's poor understanding. Hard data and good scholarship first— then on to stage 2:
2. Personal synthesis of what is discovered based on a personal sense of Beauty.
3. Enactment of that synthesis.
4. Sharing the results of stage three with those who are part of his or her School.

The daemonic level arises from the past Formulas for what has worked, and how. The Symbol for the daemonic level is the Scroll.

Each of these four parts of the cosmos must be explored, manipulated, learned from, and reshaped by the Left Hand Path practitioner to the glory of his or her Satanic Will. Some will find certain levels easy to tap into, others difficult. Since the Left Hand Path is centered on the self, there is always the temptation not to enter into exchange with these levels, to be some sort of vampire that merely tries to absorb without giving. Such pathetic creatures may obtain a certain level of power in this world, but they remain small and twisted, they can not partake of the fullness of being that fair exchange allows. To work with the surface, you must dedicate yourself to those causes in the world that increase human freedom and potential. To work with the medial level, you must engage yourself in

12

creation of such medial artifacts that increase human awareness. To work with the core level, you must lead a life that serves as a model of self-development. To work with the daemonic level, you must share the results of your research and experiments with others who are striving in the direction of the mysteries.

These eight levels of being, four internal and four external, are joined together by the act of Perception. This process requires not merely "looking" at things, but preparing yourself to see them— which may mean education, or getting rid of emotional baggage, or learning occult techniques. Perception beckons energy from the outer realms, and directs it into the inner realms. It is the source of nourishment, and as it improves by practice and the removal of delusion, it becomes the basis for unifying the Self in such a manner that coherent afterlife states are possible.

The Psychology of Initiation

Initiation is the process of self change. It involves discovering what inherent patterns of the Self exist and manipulating one's life circumstance, learning, and action so that those patterns may reach their fullest potential and be freely and creatively exercised. In many ways, initiation may be called "the process of thinking the right thought at the right time."

The inherent patterns of the core self are sometimes confused with Right Hand Path concepts like "destiny" or "fate." The Right Hand Path looks for pathways for the self to submit to, whereas the Left Hand Path seeker looks for pathways to grow in. The core self, like an acorn, has certain potentials, but just as most acorns do not grow into mighty oaks, so too most core selves never obtain any realization.

We will look first at the stages of initiation, then the vices and virtues of initiation, and lastly what initiation means in the current world.

Initiation consists of seven stages. Each has its rules. This is a simplified version of life; real life is sometimes harder to divide into acts than a play.

The first stage is that of *wandering*. The initiate-to-be moves around the world according to the circumstances of their birth and guided by the intervention of their daemonic self. He or she will see many things, meet many people, have many experiences. This material is acquired during a time of great naiveté — the initiate believes that surface appearances are true. Humans are good, those in authority know more than the rest of us, people wearing black hats are evil. The beliefs that rule the initiate-to-be are gathered at random; sometimes they are very noble such as a belief in human's ability to help themselves, sometimes very base such as racism. Those humans, roughly five percent of humanity (of every color, sex, sex preference) that have the capacity to avoid regression go through this phase. (When most people meet a new and stressful environment, they regress into a more primitive behavior such as drinking, or sleeping a lot, and so forth— only about five percent use the stress to move them into a more complex system of behavior.) This continues until stage two.

The second stage is *shock*. Something happens demonstrating the falsity of appearances. A lover is unfaithful, the government pulls you out of school because of a quota, you are much less smart than everyone told you were in the small town you grew up in, etc. The nature of the shock is unique to the person. It does however knock them off the path of life they were following. Many people don't have this occur; they are not marked to be initiates, but the allies of initiates. Most people never recover from this shock. They fall deeply asleep; their only magical function is to have children and pass along such daemonic material they may have in the form of family spirits and so forth. The Initiate, however, does not fall completely asleep.

The third stage is *daydreaming*. The Initiate begins a regression into a fantasy world while they rebuild their life. Driven by desires awakened above, they seek out those things that are resonant with those desires. They dabble in occultism, play at alternative lifestyles, and generally restructure the medial parts of themselves with the idea of "What if?" Most people remain at that level. They make up the coffee house crowd in every city, the people that go to cool movies, and otherwise the market that magicians make their money off of. However some of these folk are overtaken by desire, and begin to break out of the economic (and/or socially-constructed) cage holding them. They try their hand at starting a band, or at writing, or at starting a business, or at organizing a political or cultural group. They have success despite the odds against them. They discover that things are possible if they are Willed. They put "Follow your bliss!" bumper stickers on their van, and are truly quite puzzled why more people don't do as they do. These folk are the salt of the earth and many Left Hand Path initiates will tear their hair wondering why these folk, who have taken a step or two on the path, don't fully awaken. But some of them do. Usually some sorcerous skills are developed here such as obtainment through visualization and autohypnosis.

The fourth stage is another *shock*. Here the Initiate discovers that there are great possibilities outside of the life they currently lead. This can happen in differing ways; they may read a book on the effect of the occult on history, or they may meet a talented magician, or they may have some manifestation of their own daemonic self. Here is a time of great danger. Now that the individual knows the world does not work in ways either explained fully in rational science, nor is the human world organized as mainstream media would have you believe — there is a tendency to throw away logic and reason, and obsess on bizarre explanations of the world, whether it manifests as an over-interest in conspiracies, UFOs, or diet fads. However in some lucky few the powers of skepticism and their daemonic selves are balanced so that they can find a School. Those lost at this level of Shock spend their days tearing at the social fabric.

The fifth stage is the *School*. A School consists of four elements. First it must have a consistent metaphysics, that is to say, a system of thought that contains ethics, ontology, epistemology, and praxis. Second it must have Teachers, living men and women who have bettered themselves by applying the School's ideas in a variety of real-life circumstances, and whose struggles must be similar to the Seeker's. Third it must have a variety of students from as large a range of walks of life, nationalities, cultures, and so forth as possible. This allows that the system can be tested

14

in many differing ways. Fourth the School must provide resistance, a graduated steps of mastery based on objective criteria, so that the student is receiving something other than simple messages about how grand he or she is.

If the chemistry between the School and the Seeker is correct — in other words, if the School provides enough challenge and friction coupled with enough useful Knowledge, and the Seeker provides magical curiosity and hard work — then the Seeker may awaken, and all the aspects of his or her life can be enriched thereby. Such Seekers then become fiercely protective of the School and, by their being, an advertisement for it.

In connecting with the Teacher, the student begins by projecting all of the qualities that the student wants onto the Teacher. Now if it so happens that such qualities are part of the Teacher's makeup, then a magical process of Learning begins as well as the mundane process.

As the student comes to a certain state of being, their Strivings enable them to contact the Teacher within. This is the sign of a true School. At this point the School becomes a place of resources and networking as the Student uses its members as fellow researchers around the world. This is a type of empowerment that opens as many doors as magical practice does.

Some Students pass into direct interaction with the Prince of Darkness through a method akin to the one they used from passing from human Teacher to the Teacher within. At this point the School becomes a place for them to share their techniques of Awakening.

However no School is as good as its idealized model, which leads to the next phase:

The sixth stage is yet another *shock*. Here the Student learns that his or her Teachers are in the long run just people like him- or herself. They see the great tragedy of Initiation, which is that when Initiates screw up, they do so on a grander scale than regular folk. This leads them to various deflections of Initiation. They may decide that their Teacher is "corrupt" or that Initiation is just an illusion, or worse still they may decide that they have license to pursue such petty evils as they may see (or imagine) others "above" them practice. Here the very Sovereignty they have been seeking is abdicated by their interest in the weakness of others, rather than in preserving and increasing their own strength. But those who survive this shock pass onto the last phase of Initiation.

The seventh stage is *Work*. Here the Initiate takes on the issue of world change. They usually maintain a fraternal and magical link to their School, and a presence in the various communities that fostered their coming into being. This Loyalty to one's own past is the way that Initiates in this stage of life maintain their Awareness. They rise to the top of their chosen fields of endeavor, create a life that is uniquely satisfying to them, and finish the self-change issues that have been part of their process since the first stage of Initiation. At the end of their life, they work on simplifying and purifying their experience, so that they can pass on the rules of life to their apprentices in their trade, the fellow Students in their School, and their descendants. This is the last bringing out of the materials of their soul to work in the world; it is not a Gift to their loved ones, but a means of keeping their impulses alive on earth as they prepare for the shock of death and the states beyond.

It should be noted that just as some of these stages may overlap temporally (or in rare cases, not proceed in this order) the "shocks" need not be single events, but clusters of events occurring over days, months, or even years. Even death may not occur as a single event, but a series of events of physical and mental decline.

The Vices and Virtues of Initiation

Vices are those habits of mind, heart, and will that hold us back from our self-determined goals. They can be eliminated by analyzing the behaviors that support them and cutting away those behaviors. Virtues are those qualities of mind, heart, and will that lead to an increase of Being. They can be learned by studying the actions of those who possess these attributes and emulating them.

The Vices

1. Narcissism. Because the Left Hand Path focuses on the Self, there is a sad tendency to see the self as an object of worship. This is as useful as if a sculptor began to worship clay. The Initiate guards against this with humor, willingness to apologize, and asking himself the question about any bad situation he or she finds themselves in, "How did my actions contribute to this jam?"

2. Hubris. Because the LHP Initiate does have access to mental states that 99.99% of his fellow humans do not, he can come to believe that all of his actions are justified. He may even come to believe that the Truths he has come to by the practice of Initiatory magic are universal Truths, becoming the same sort of bigot he fled from early in his life. The cure for hubris is to associate with powerful, smart people that make you aware of how little you know, and how much more room there is for achievement in your life. The LHP initiate shuns being a big fish in a small pond.

3. Forgetfulness of past orthodoxies. Since we come to a surface level (or some would say intellectual) understanding of the fettering power of Right Hand Path thought, we often think that we are "over it." Those channels are cut very deep in our medial selves, just as they are in the world. If we do not understand this, we will inevitably return to the bad habits of thought that we despised. The victim of the religious bigot will become a religious bigot. The former Christian will come to believe in a loving Prince of Darkness. The former skeptic will disbelieve even the results of his own magic and preach against it. The LHP Initiate tests (and asks those in his or her life to test) whether or not she or he is showing the bad thought-patterns of their past.

4. Despair. Because of the immensity of the task of self-change, it is very easy to be overcome with despair. Once this happens, initiation stops. The Initiate must learn how to keep a certain amount of pleasurable challenge in his or her life at all times, so that fun — as much as anything else — will draw them back into initiatory practice.

5. Attachment to the thoughts of another. When you have had your eyes opened to the fact that the world is very different than society would have you believe, it is very tempting to embrace the first coherent thought system you encounter. People may pick Crowley, Gurdjieff, Plato, Sartre, Whitehead, or some nut on Access TV that channels kazillion-year-old Lemurians, but in each case they have stopped thinking on their own, and replaced thought with a language game that requires memory and repetition. The LHP Initiate will look at all these things with a bit of a mental force-field in place, saying to him- or herself, "Well that might be helpful for me, but what do I think about it?"

6. Obsession with Magic. Magic, which is ultimately the manipulation of the mind, is very entertaining— so much so that it can eat someone's life away as much as TV or surfing the Net. The Left Hand Path magician holds this tendency at bay with the use of a magical diary that integrates each magical operation into the overall scheme of his life.

7. Emotional servitude. Many would-be writers write only when "the mood is right." Many would-be Initiates only take care of their Initiation when "the mood is right." In both cases people don't learn their craft, and they don't have the hard and painful breakthroughs that are as important as the easy "Aha" breakthroughs. The Left Hand Path Initiate knows that he or she doesn't follow his or her emotions, but that his emotions follow him. He or she practices doing things that are difficult for the sheer power it gives them over their emotions.

The Virtues

1. Magical Curiosity. The daemonic level of the world is maintained by the actions of coherent and transformative systems. These are seldom the systems you can learn about in an occult bookstore. If true Secrets were found in such places, then your fellow customers would be the most powerful people on Earth. The true systems may have their broad outlines available there, but the hard work of finding out how these things really work is the Initiate's job. Their quest for Knowledge will lead them into truly hidden areas, that may require pilgrimages to ancient sites, research in dusty libraries, or picking up a few additional languages. The occult industry, which is based on a few books about everything under the sun, hates this sort of Seeker (after he or she has paid back the occult world by doing a couple of general books on the topic). The LHP Initiate knows that each answer leads to nine more questions— and the quest of getting those answers IS the very Path itself.

2. Quantifiable Pride. We live in a world that is very short on recognition. People are afraid to recognize quality. It might empower a rival, or make them aware of their own lack of achievement. Yet as humans we long for recognition. So the LHP Initiate does speak of his or her real-world deeds. But in order to avoid the traps of egotism they use a certain formula. They mention the real deed, and then link it to the next real-world achievement they are striving for. For example, "Last semester I made the Dean's list; next semester I will get into the doctoral program." This type of formula has four effects. First it lets people know that you are a force in the world,

17

and they will treat you accordingly. Second it will plant an image in their minds of your success, so that they will be unconsciously working magic for you to succeed. Third it lets you know that you are a person of real worth, and fourth it reminds you of how far you need to go in order to achieve your long-range goals.

3. Sense of Humor. If an Initiate can not laugh at his or her own mistakes, they should give up trying. If they can't laugh at the world, they will go mad. Laughter is the banisher of obsessions, and the mark of someone sure of their Sovereignty.

4. Openness. Many people are so insecure that they lead lives so tight that magic couldn't break in even if from the Prince of Darkness Itself. They have rules about what to eat, when to sleep, who to fuck, what to read, how to vote — until every second of their life is filled. The LHP Initiate because of faith that his or her magic will open Doors for them, tries new things, and is very spontaneous. True development will come to someone with Will-To-Succeed long before it will come to someone with Will-To-Control.

5. Moderation. The Sovereign Self knows that nothing outside of itself is essential, nor is anything forbidden. Therefore it refuses those paths and people that have "one is the right way" attitude. It chooses between libertinage and asceticism, knowing that each is a distortion of the self. Neither addiction nor abstinence are answers of a person that rules his or her life.

6. Synthesis. The late Anton S. La Vey was ahead of the game at this. He took useful aspects of life from a variety of sources — photography, fiction, sexology, and so forth — to form his system. The LHP Initiate looks for his tools in a variety of life experiences, and does not draw all of his or her practice from the occult world.

7. Cunning. The Left Hand Path Initiate always has an ace in the hole for any situation. He or she does not put all of his eggs in one basket. He or she has cunning, a type of knowing and thought formed by a complex but coherent constellation of attitudes and skills which combine flair, extensive networking, wisdom, forethought, subtlety of mind, deception, observation of people's nonverbal cues, resourcefulness, vigilance, opportunism, and various skills and experience acquired over the years. It is applied to conditions which are passing, shifting, nonplusing and ambiguous, and to those magically potent situations which do not lend themselves to precise measurement, exact calculation, and rigorous logic.

What Is Needed for Initiation in the Postmodern World

In the time of our ancestors' ancestors we had Schools that were deeply connected with the culture, both on a linguistic and material culture basis, that taught Sovereignty. Some of these were closed to certain bloodlines, others like Plato's Academy were open to persons of merit. We do not exist in a small unified coherent culture. One School will not provide you with all of your Needs.

You must look not only for a School that will Teach you magic and philosophy, but for life activities that deepen your personhood. Some of these might be better colleges, field work in the sciences, special forces training in the military, careers in music or art, training in the martial arts, and so forth. Finding the tools for your self-transformation isn't easy.

If you come across any School that claims it has all you need, run — don't walk — away.

Schools should be hard to get into; Schools should stress that your battlefield is your life, not your memory skills; Schools should encourage your meeting the instructors face-to-face.

The Nature of Magic

Magic consists of pulling things from the Darkness into the Light. Darkness is the realm of potential existence. It may be understood as the future, the repressed, the hidden, or the forbidden.

If you lacked a job one night, did a ritual, and got the job, you pulled it out of the Darkness.

It came. But it came with mysterious properties that you had to experience to know. Coming to know those properties will provide you with self knowledge.

If you overcome some neurosis that didn't let you form lasting commitments to persons of the appropriate sex, you have pulled commitment out of Darkness.

This will allow you to have a long-term lover, which is perhaps the greatest aid to traveling along the Path.

If you caused your government to reveal a secret that it had been using against its citizens, you have pulled that secret from the Darkness.

This will set up for new conditions of freedom in the world.

If you made your long-standing sexual fantasy into flesh with two or three willing adult partners, you have pulled it from the Darkness.

This will accustom you to the process of Dreams becoming Flesh.

Magic is the art or science of causing change in the microcosm so the proportionate change may occur in the macrocosm, depending on the precision and passion of the magician. It is how we get what we Need.

There are four sorts of magic. They are Metacommunication, Sorcery, Divination, and Initiatory magic. Each takes a lifetime to master, and each can be a useful tool in both improving the circumstances of life and integrating and developing the self. Let us look at each:

Metacommunication

Metacommunication includes any sending of a message that is more than what it seems.

We practice Metacommunication for four reasons. First, to achieve goals that normal channels of communication won't allow us. Second, to enchant our lives. Third, to learn to lessen the effect of Metacommunication upon us. Fourth, to produce internal friction and Awareness of Purpose. Let's look at each of these and then at the dangers of Metacommunication.

To achieve goals that normal channels of communication won't allow us. As Magicians we strive to change the world around us to allow for

19

more freedom and more opportunity. The way of the world does not support Freedom and Opportunity. The way of the world is to insist on its rules.

To enchant our lives. We practice Metacommunication for fun. We may practice it by telling a ghost story around a campfire, spinning a tall tale to a fellow airline passenger, telling a sick friend that the tea you are giving them has magical powers that will make them feel better, or even giving that special someone a fortune cookie whose fortune happens to read, "Will you marry me?"

To lessen the effects of Metacommunication on us. The world has a constant barrage of signals coming our way. A very small percentage is challenged by our consciousness. The rest just pours in. How many of you have tried to clear your mind and found that there was a Pepsi Cola advertisement running there? We will always be amateurs at Metacommunication compared to Madison Avenue, but we will be armed amateurs.

To produce internal friction and Awareness of Purpose. The single greatest weakness of the Left Hand Path Initiate is egotism. Usually it is in the form of a semiautonomous part of the psyche that justifies all past action. In Metacommunication situations you have to learn not to talk all the time, not to let everyone know your every little thought, and spend more time listening than broadcasting; you learn your big purpose comes first. The person who knows she must rent the house for X dollars can screen out the chatter of the real estate agent— and by acting rather then reacting, get her Wish, as well as get training of the Will.

The danger in Metacommunication is that it is seductive. It can allow us to transform a hard situation where we might Learn something into an easy situation where we will not, it can allow us to cheapen a relationship based on Truth into one based on manipulation, it can begin to tarnish the way we look at our fellow humans. Because of this a strong ethical background is needed.

Sorcery

Sorcery is the manipulation of matter and words to effect a change in the world. Using a voodoo doll to get rid of an enemy, creating a money-drawing fetish, or healing the sick by use of an enchantment are examples of sorcery. Sorcery requires a certain amount of native talent, a good deal of emotional energy, a playful attitude, and a scientific approach to see what works.

Native talent is the expression of your daemonic self. If you have ever had a "miracle" that pulled you out of a bad situation, you have talent for sorcery.

Emotional energy is the key to this sort of magical working. You must not only raise your emotional energy to the maximum level during the work, you have to send it forth beyond you. In other words, you not only have to have a great deal of passion at your disposal, you have to be able to let things go. If you can't walk away from your magical operation feeling that you have taken care of the situation, you won't be able to work sorcery.

A playful attitude allows you to perform such work. You must be willing to see aspects of the outer world, such as your voodoo doll, as true stand-ins for the thing you wish to influence. Logic and reason, which are normally the best tools for acquiring power in the world, must be dropped for the time of your ceremony, then picked up again as your life resumes its normal workaday course.

A scientific approach to see what works is essential in developing your powers. You must note your operation, see when and if it took effect, and what unexpected side effects occurred. This way you will learn what you are good at, what doesn't work for you, how the world is connected (for example, did you want to heal that woman who then took your boyfriend away?) and what you really want, and Need.

Sorcery has two advantages and two dangers. It tells you how good you are at magic, and how quickly (or slowly) your magic works. This is important knowledge to have in your possession before you try any Initiatory magic. You wouldn't want to do brain surgery if you're not sure you know how to put on a bandage. The second benefit is that sorcery can get you many things— if you learn how to ask for them. If you are good at magic, you get what you ask for— most people learn that the hard way! One disadvantage of sorcery is that it can easily lure you into far too comfortable a life. You hex people you don't like, you do a money spell that keeps you in your crappy little apartment, you manage to keep pain out of your mouth so you go too long before you see a dentist. The second disadvantage of sorcery is that it will lead (everyone goes through this once, folks!) to the Sorcerer's Apprentice Syndrome. In the SAS, you get into a spiral of magically-aided disasters. It goes something like this. Al puts a spell on that cute woman at work. She falls for him in a big way, and it isn't till after weeks of great sex that Al discovers that she is a psychopath. No problem: Al does a spell that will take her away from his place of employment. The company goes belly-up. Everyone is now away from the place of employment. Al needing cash does a "Get Me Moola Quick" ritual, and is struck by a BMW, whose owner wants to settle fast. And so on.

Modern sorcerers would do well to study chaos theory to discover why sometimes things work, sometimes they don't. Eventually as one comes to know more and more about what is possible in the world, a sense of timing will develop for your sorcery. Learning to take that secret of timing to the rest of your life is a major Initiatory leap forward.

Here's an example of sorcery:

Practical Sigil Construction

There is something special about Sigil magic. Magic is the Art of communication, where you send or receive signals from the hidden part of the universe. Some people are very sensitive to magic, others very resistant. Some are good at sending signals, so they need very little effort to power things; others have to take every bit of emotion, power, and

21

passion they have to get anything going. The direct use of signs is one of the easiest and most powerful methods of magic.

The sign can be manipulated. It can be painted, burned, coated with sexual fluids, carved in rock, cast in metal. Each of these things creates a meta-message about what you want the sign to do. A sign for a temporary purpose, like "make my neighbor fall in love with me" is not something you want carved in stone. A sign to bring you good health on the other hand would logically be created out of something that will be around as long as you are. Plastic maybe.

There are many symbol systems that you can use to create Sigils. The runes, the Hebrew alphabet, you name it.

I am going to show how to create a Sigil in a method that is entirely personal. It is unique to you, and therefore has about it a certain Left Hand Path resonance. All Left Hand Path practitioners should develop a personal magical system unique to themselves as part of their self development.

To begin you will need a magic square. Now English has 26 letters, which doesn't work so well, but if you choose to treat two of them as the same — say I and J or I and Y — then you have 25 letters which makes a nice 5-by-5 square.

First you will need a magic phrase unique to your current level of understanding and your wants. Let's say your current magical motto is "I will grow by overcoming fear!" When one communicates something in the intellectual realm, one strives for simple, clear sentences that either persuade or explain. A magician wishing to communicate his will to the essentially mysterious parts of his own psyche utilizes a precise method of transporting his message from the intellectual to the daemonic realm. What follows is a simple method. Note that it does not coerce some other being — such as an angel or demon or other fantasy — but rather assumes that the daemonic part of the magician is willing to work for the same purpose as the magician.

This system uses component letters of a phrase to produce a shape through which the will of the magician can operate directly upon the worlds within and without. Let's take the unique letters in that phrase, treating Y as I, and discarding duplicate letters, to produce: I W L G R O B V E C M N F A. Let's fill up our square with those letters first,

I	W	L	G	R
O	B	V	E	C
M	N	F	A	

Now we'll fill it in with the other letters of the alphabet:

I	W	L	G	R
O	B	V	E	C
M	N	F	A	D
H	J	K	P	Q
S	T	U	X	Z

Now this is your magic square. Let's take a particular intention that crosses your mind. Do you need a new job, because the money will help you do things like get a better education? Are you afraid of the new job however? Seems to fit into your overall purpose. So construct a sentence, "Job, challenge, and money are mine!" Now reduce that to its unique letters, J O B C H A L E N G D M I. (With I as both I an Y).

Now make a nice angular drawing that connects each of the letters in order. It should look something like this:

Look it over, does it seem right? Nice how it looks like spiraling inverted pentagrams. Put your magic square away, and Play with your Sigil. Load it with power, keep it on your person when you write up your resume. It is a thousand times more valid than a Sigil from some musty grimoire. When it has done its Work, offer it up as a sacrifice to your Higher Self. And while the little piece of paper burns say words of Pledge to yourself that you will use the new job to Learn as well as earn, and that you accept the pleasure and pains your magic has brought you, as your hard work opens new fields for your Xeper.

Dont show others your magical square, any more than you would share your PIN for your ATM card. The Sigils however need not be hidden, since they remain a secret in plain view.

From time to time as you evolve you will Need to change your magical square showing a new attack on the universe.

Divination

Divination is the process of discovering information about yourself, others, or the forces of the universe by means of watching signs, either those formally manipulated or synchronicities that occur around you.

The Left Hand Path Initiate practices divination for four reasons.

First and most importantly, to fill his or her life with a sense of wonder.

23

Second, to see if his or her current life path is optimal. Reason and sense of self produce the great guidelines, but divination can fine tune your course.

Third, to cause the Initiate to think about the near future, and learn those feelings and thoughts that might never had occurred to him or her. Fourth, to impress others.

The use of a Divinatory system requires four things to be of use to the Awakened Black Magician. Firstly it must reflect a Sovereign viewpoint, that is to say these are Symbols that apply to the questions of kingship, not when the crops need to be harvested. Secondly the system must be usable within a rational and ordered life. Thirdly the questioner must be of great emotional maturity. Fourthly, the system must have uses in sorcery.

Let us consider the idea of war. Now if you asked a general to write down the categories of war, he might write battles, logistics, strategy, civil affairs, morale, and so forth. If you asked a physician, her list might be shell shock, limb loss, field surgery, and the like. The lowly private might have boredom, mud, death of friends, fear. Now each of these is a complete map of war that serves the person doing the mapping. It reflects their needs, their observations, and their wisdom. The Initiate looks for a system designed by rulers, for rulers — whether it would be Crowley's Tarot deck, the Runes, the Ogham, and so forth.

If you choose to read the Divinatory system to aid/manipulate your friends, you impose upon them three things. Firstly, a viewpoint of a class to which you are becoming a member. Secondly, awe and respect for that class. Thirdly, wisdom beyond (but tempered by) your own. This moves them into a dynamism that you can manipulate in accordance with your will, and helps you realize your own consciousness in a more permanent form. This is yet another example of Left Hand Path practice — wherein you become more and more the constant, and all else the variable.

If you use the Divinatory system to help yourself out of a jam, by checking for which areas to aim your Will at, you are imposing three things upon yourself and your surroundings. Firstly, you are imposing rules for an idealized world that you would rather work in. Secondly, you are allowing your dilemma to move you toward the Judgment/Control aspect of your being. Thirdly, you are alleviating the stress of chaos by a magical and purposeful act rather than a bottle of Old Grandpa. This Divination attunes you to the Divinatory system and the world to you.

If you use the fullness of ideas expressed in the Divinatory system as a map showing where your true core self stands, you are imposing three things on yourself. Firstly, you are separating your self from the universe by the simple act of reminding yourself that you are the center of it. Secondly, you are making yourself aware of blind spots in your Initiation. If you can't see how a certain world is important as another, it reflects a lack of balance that needs to be corrected by Willed action, or will be corrected by the universe in her usual sweet and loving way. Thirdly, it reminds you of the Deeper work that needs to be done — making your own map of the Cosmos, so that you can effect it with utter precision now, and after your death. This latter exercise in Objective Consciousness is very hard.

Since the Tarot is a common divinatory tool, I will give an example of a formal divination procedure using the Tarot.

One, ask yourself these questions:

1. How does my current situation reflect possibilities for my development?
2. How have my weaknesses contributed to my being where I am? How can I use getting out of where I am to get where I need to be?
3. What will the **real** impact of my current situation be in six days, six months, and six years?
4. How many factors are governing the current situation?

Two, write down the answers in your magical diary.

Three, do an Invocation:

"Oh Self that I seek to Become, open your mysteries to me. Rejoice in steps to overcome that which hinders me, bless my serenity in accepting that which I must suffer to change me, and energize my magical curiosity that I may know the difference. Let my view extend beyond time and space! Hail, my Self-to-Be!"

Four, put out the cards and read them according to the methods you have seen used. A good historical understanding of the system is very important as well as common reading skill. For a historical understanding of the Tarot, see *The Tarok of the Magians* by Stephen Flowers.

Five, write down the reading and your interpretation of it. Be brutal with yourself.

Six, look for other patterns, things like who the cards remind you of, noises in your room, other synchronicities. Note them as well.

Seven, now pick up the cards you don't like, put down cards in their place for the reading you would like to see. Think about how you would need to change the things in your life to move toward this pattern. Keep the cards out where you can study the pattern every day for four or five days; during this time you can make a few more changes. At the end of that time say another invocation, "From the Future you come!" Leave the cards out in the Dark that night. Then begin working to make your Willed prediction come true.

Eight, write down your successes and failures.

Nine, every six or seven months review your progress. Are you becoming more accurate with your predictions? (If not, try a different system.) Are you becoming better at bringing about what you want? (If not, examine your life very carefully.)

This procedure reflects a Left Hand Path use of an existing occult technology. It is, of course, much harder than the occult world would teach you, but it is also more useful.

Initiatory Magic

Initiatory magic is the Creating/Preserving of a desired Perception. It is the Secret of the Magi. As we struggle in the world to understand, to be strong and virtuous, to become what we desire, we have the very tough job of building up our virtue bit by bit. Each hard act gives us so little, and a lifetime of laziness and blindness will often remove such small treasures as we may have. Initiatory magic is changing oneself to give the desired traits a foothold in the darkness of the psyche. It is like planting a seed.

Initiatory magic is of two kinds, that related to social rites of passage, and that which is done by the magician for his or her inner agenda. The first sort is ceremonies of graduation, weddings, funerals. These belong to the outer world, and it is up to the Awakened Will of the Initiate to make use of them. That is her or his duty (and the following steps are just as applicable). The second sort, the inner-directed magic, may be done alone or in groups dedicated to Initiation. This is the process whereby a change is wrought in Perception, which may be brought to bear on any or all of the four levels of microcosmic dynamism, or (more rarely) on the levels of macrocosmic dynamism.

Now both sorts of magic are present in the life of the Initiate. Let us consider what the Initiate's attitude toward them should be. External Initiatory magic has been the method by which society and family have shaped the Initiate's world view, given him or her values, and created semi-stable structures in the various dynamisms of him- or herself. Immature LHP philosophies suggest that such things are merely to be hated and inverted. Mature philosophies look at the results and then make their Pact with mankind. Let's say that you are a white male from the American South of a lower middle class family, and of Irish descent. There will be certain things you have gained through ritual and myth: a sense of honor, a romantic view of human achievement, racism, religious intolerance, a tendency to enjoy loafing. Instead of hating this force that made you, marvel at it— take its products and enforce those you like (sense of honor) and toss away those that hinder you (racism). Do this within and without, and engage in those rituals which promote those values you value. This is our Pact with mankind. Internal Initiatory magic needs to be viewed as very serious and productive of Unknown consequences. Most of the occult industry is full of books that allow you to be "initiated" into system after system. The LHP Initiate knows that if their rites are working at all, it is not unlike switching on every light and appliance in his house— eventually the circuits will blow, after a brownout. Initiatory magic must only be practiced when there is Need, a true obstacle in your inner being that must be overcome quickly rather then slowly and permanently.

The steps for Initiatory magic are four: Purification, Intensification, Consummation, and Realization. Let's look at each of these.

Purification. This is not a process of avoiding sex or chocolate. It is a process of mental purification. It requires two things. Firstly building up a great sense of question. The Initiate takes on every aspect of the question facing him or her. He thinks about it, entertains wild speculations, uses his logic, uses divination and other methods for getting beyond his head, reads philosophers, discusses the idea with wise people of varying viewpoints.

Secondly it requires the Initiate shutting out those worldly influences that will distract him or her during the actual performance. For most people it means stop reading the newspapers, watching TV, or surfing the web for a couple of days before the work. It might mean sleeping alone the day before and after the magical working, and avoiding such foods that dull the senses. It certainly means avoiding alcohol and drugs before the work.

Intensification. This is a process of fixing one's senses on such items and stimuli that aid in creating the atmosphere. It means choice of art, clothing, music, and other aesthetic decisions. This process allow the consciousness to slip upward toward a divine level. This state is the state sought by the Left Hand Path, and such glimpses as occur during Initiatory magic are a sort of travelogue for the soul. The ultimate aim of the Left Hand Path — an immortal consciousness that can act or not in the material world as desired — is seen here.

Consummation. Here the desired new state is taken in by symbolic actions. The external condensation of the mental state could be as simple as a drink of apple juice from a goblet, Symbolizing the gaining of Wisdom. This state uses the body for the Mind to Work on the Mind. The change is wrought here, and will begin to manifest in the four inner and four outer levels.

Realization. Initiatory magic does not improve character. You will not walk out of a magical chamber a new man or woman; although the changes wrought in your inner world will make it *feel* so. So the Initiate plans to engage in some activity the next day that illustrates the desired state. If the ritual was to obtain Lore, the Realization is going to class on Mythology the next day. This aligning of outer action with an internally wrought change is almost a Secret of the Left Hand Path. Real world change is always the test of our magic.

Why Magic Is Taught

The intelligent seeker now has a question as to why these types of magic are taught. If I (or anyone) really had the secret for doing things that other people could not, wouldn't it be to my advantage keeping this knowledge to myself?

There are seven reasons why magic is taught:

1. It's fun to show off what you know. This is hard-wired biology of the human species, it makes for the survival of the race. Our aging process feeds this, which is why people of a certain age desire to pass on information to youth. The Initiate, who studies always the chemistry of Life, uses this Chemistry rather then struggles against it.

2. It binds Perception to the Left Hand Path. The Prince of Darkness gave us the Gift of Individuality so that he could in the fullness of time have suitable companions. One of the ways we link with that Cosmic Working is to make sure that the Left Hand Path survives. By being able to look upon our students, we know that we have affected the psyches of others as the Prince of Darkness affected ours, and this Knowledge aids the soul in its crystallization.

27

3. It brings new techniques forward. As seekers for the modern Left Hand Path arrive drawn by this Teaching, they bring a lifetime of wandering to the Teacher. They will have encountered some drops of wisdom on the way, otherwise they would never have had enough Being to be drawn to the Teaching. These may be added to the School's horde, after testing and evaluation. True Initiatory Schools, rather then trying to Teach everyone everything, actually become places where Wisdom is gathered. In the early days of a new School great wisdom comes in daily, so many new groups flourish for a while, but as a certain level of Transformation occurs in the group, it becomes rarer and rarer that each new bit of Knowledge will be as Transformative.

4. It articulates the Teaching. If you really, really want to learn something — from French to computer programming — try teaching it.

5. It brings money and fame, which can be used for a variety of purposes.

6. It increases the amount of the Unknown in the universe. In the world of Right Hand Path religions, the Known is sought. Everything should be fixed, and the chaotic driven from the world. In the Left Hand Path, as individuals evolve in their unique fashion, in their personal time and using those materials of time of culture where ever they are— a growing number of questions arise (since each Answer leads to nine questions) and a growing individuation of the divine occurs. Rather than producing more of the Known, this produces the Unknown. It is in this atmosphere that more consciousness can evolve, and the evolving consciousness will have more opportunities for power and development in the world.

7. It frees the Teacher from the social matrix. Sure we know what to do with plumbers, rock stars, gym teachers, jewelers, and bank tellers. But what do you do with a Magician? Is he to be treated with respect or derision? Is she rich or poor? Is he conservative or liberal? By cutting him- or herself from the social matrix the Teacher of magic has set up a situation where he has to stay Awake, but she has also created a situation where it is easier to Work her Will on the world.

Historical and Cultural Opportunities for the Left Hand Path

The Left Hand Path is at the dawn of a new era of sophistication and power. This does not mean that it will be easier, nor more socially acceptable to practice, but that the practice can have greater effect. Let us consider the development of the world so far, and then look at why the Postmodern or Aeonic Age will prove to be the Golden Era of LHP practice.

World history has passed through three great epochs and is passing into a fourth.

In classical times we had great growth of many paradigms. This led to great schools of philosophical inquiry. We would be hard pressed to look at the philosophies of ancient Greece alone, and think that we have made any progress toward Knowing the answers of the questions posed by Life. But two things were lacking: One, a system of universals that allowed philosophies to be taught, exchanged, improved across the boundaries of time and space. Two, a useful knowledge of the material world that could empower the philosophic seeker to realize his or her Ideas in the world.

In medieval times we had one paradigm. One god, one book, one initiation across racial and cultural lines. This produced many good things: A realization of the need of a common language (then Latin, now English), common time keeping, rules for international travel. In short in the Middle Ages the design for a set of common factors that enabled the Word to go forth from Rome, or Mecca, or Constantinople, or Beijing created the Idea of a common basis for communication and control.

In modern times the paradigm of science — of approaching the world rationally as a way of controlling it — has given us many things. We live twice as long as we used to— pretty important if you are going to spend time figuring out the answers to life's questions. We can travel almost anywhere in a short period of time. We can interact with other minds in a moment. The power of the individual is at an all-time summit because of science, but because of human beings' natural laziness this power is usually turned against the Self, as we learn new ways to keep ourselves distracted.

The Postmodern or Aeonic Age could be the synthesis of the three preceding. It will have the growth of many, many paradigms for inquiry. These will be communicated by universal means, from books to the Internet. They will be empowered by the mastery of the natural science makes possible. In such a time, the inspired book of another will matter less, because the most important acquisition of the individual will be a philosophy system that helps him or her utilize the historical forces that are coming into being now.

If we speak of the "world" of Thomas Jefferson or the "world" of Einstein, we are talking about a set of mental attitudes and ways of knowing that make the Cosmos clear, usable, and give direction for its use. These sets of attitude have been determined by external forces, upon which there has been a dependency (*e.g.,* medieval churches or modern governments) up to the present, but with the new technologies and the revolt of the elites, intelligent people are able to find their own worlds. Entrance into one of the Aeons has a fourfold effect. Firstly the individual feels like they have found "home." This is a brief Remembering of their true nature. Secondly the individual finds other people to explore the ideas with. This is the forming of an elite. *Any* Aeon is Ruled by its elite. The elites have been agents of Dependency until recently when their actions have become both more global in scope and self centered in mood. Thirdly the individual finds that the Aeon empowers him as he quests for its Secrets. Fourthly the individual finds that the quest leads to him or her either making significant improvements to the Aeon, or founding one of his or her own.

This paradigm of the acquisition of knowledge and power is a Left Hand Path paradigm; although it can be used in non-spiritual pursuits. As this method becomes the ruling method, the Left Hand Path magician will find himself more deeply in Resonance with the Medial, Core, and Daemonic levels of the world, and his or her activities will be greatly amplified.

Another benefit that the Left Hand Path Initiate can now enjoy is a growing tolerance in this age for individual beliefs. Although the intolerance of other ages does not vanish (if you doubt me, watch Access TV and you will see that the Middle Ages is alive and well), the newer freedoms allow for greater diversity, if one but has the will to claim one's niche. This allows for a synergy of Left Hand Path practitioners. Whereas such a group of individuals will never be in agreement on all issues, basic aims of the Left Hand Path will tend to flourish under the enlightened action of the armies of the night.

The practice of politics, the art of the possible, is where the synergy of the Left Hand Path may be brought into play during the Aeonic Age.

On the political level the Left Hand Path Initiate strives to increase four areas in her or his life: Freedom, Access to Knowledge, Scope and Nature of Opportunity, and Beauty of Environment. Let us examine each of these briefly:

Freedom is the state where the Initiate is faced by choices that will determine future states of being. Freedom does not mean choices between two types of soda, it means difficult choices that shape the self as much as a chisel shapes marble.

Access to Knowledge is the ability to find both living teachers and those treasuries of data where the products of the human mind are kept. An essential aspect of Left Hand Path philosophy is taking inventory of what is available in the Self and the environment for self creation. The use of existing material, rather than having to create each form of knowledge by the self, is essential.

Scope and Nature of Opportunity is the Left Hand Path quest for power and creativity. Initiates pride themselves on those new ideas and practices that they bring to the world. This is a form of the LHP ideal of self-deification. This form of enlivened self interest has as its goal the transformation of the business of life from a grueling job to a species of play.

Beauty of Environment is not simply sought by the Initiate for hedonistic/aesthetic reasons. For magical reasons the LHP Initiate surrounds her- or himself with those objects, sounds, works of art that remind him or her *of what she or he is seeking to become.* This practice of beautifying the world as a form of aesthetic talisman, aids the Initiate in his or her quest to become more awake and more conscious of that which they are trying to shape themselves as.

Now each of these endeavors becomes ethical in that the Left Hand Path Initiate must strive for others around him or her to achieve these things as well. This behavior is not done out of "altruism," which Left Hand Path Initiates understand as a "sacred lie" told to members of conventional religions in order to ensure their social conformity (and monetary support) in the lack of being able to make true ethical decisions based on self-gained wisdom. These cooperative strivings are done for a twofold reason: 1. Magically if one is to work with a Principle on earth, one must identify with what that Principle would find pleasing. 2. Practically each of these fields works only in opening the door for the many, not just the self.

Freedom can only be had if others are free. Working toward "total power" over others is as chaining as allowing others to have power over you. Dictators and tyrants aren't free people, merely busy ones.

The Right Hand Path

The Right Hand Path is based on the word "Submission." The guide for happiness, doing the Good, knowing the value of things comes from finding a system external to the Self, and remodeling the Self to fit. This system may take the form of obedience to an idealized being such as the Christian god, obedience to perceived historical and economic forces (*e.g.*, Marxism), obedience to a gender group (*e.g.*, feminism), obedience to a racial, national, or ethnic group.

In each instance the Other is perceived of as larger and better than the Self, and that only in service to this external principle can the Good be obtained.

The practitioners of the Right Hand Path can be noble, good men and women who chose their principles wisely (*e.g.*, Martin Luther King or Winston Churchill) or they may be destructive and stupid folk who chose their principles badly (*e.g.*, Adolf Hitler or Joseph Stalin).

The Right Hand Path is much easier to understand and explain, because it values rules over consciousness. You can find a simple text that tells you what to do.

Its concept of the divine is to see the divine as omnipotent and omnipresent. Man is but a worm in comparison, and the purpose of life is to realize how small, frail, and ultimately illusory we are.

God is seen as static, and salvation comes from achieving a similar static state, whether it is the constant adoration of the Christian heaven, or the selfless contemplation of the Buddhist Nirvana.

Many of the magical and spiritual techniques that are used by Left Hand Path Initiates are used by their RHP brothers. There are many similarities in the paths— each would stress that surface appearances in the world are misleading, each would stress that most people in the world are profoundly asleep and spend most of their energy making sure that *no one* wakes up, each would stress that the battle to change the Self is an everyday battle.

There are many religions that fall outside of the Left Hand Path/Right Hand Path dichotomy. Most folk religions are not interested in transforming the self, they are only interested in the maintenance of society. Other modes of thought such as Taoism, or Thelema as Aleister Crowley understood it, either ask different sorts of questions on how the Good is to be obtained, or offer mixtures between the paths.

There is no hatred of the Right Hand Path groups or practices by the mature Left Hand Path Initiate. The Initiate will have had to go through a break with that Path, but sees the Right Hand Path as necessary for maintaining social controls. The Initiate has to accept the hatred and mindless loathing of the less developed of the Right Hand Path practitioners, with a constant truth before him or her, "If I fall back asleep, I will be the same!" This allows even the ugly face of the RHP to be a spur to maintaining one's Awareness.

31

Chapter Two

Practice

This chapter will introduce you to the practices that maintain Awareness and foster development along the Left Hand Path. The Left Hand Path, because of its individual nature requires constant self guidance. It is harder to train oneself than to have a trainer.

There are 19 methods listed. The first two have to be done first. The remainder may be done in any logical order, based on the Needs and circumstances of the Initiate.

If you persevere and learn to enact these techniques, you will in time become completely self-directing. This is a ladder that many of you will climb and then throw away. It is important to remember your climb, so that when you reach the top, you don't destroy the Path for others by explaining how easy it us. Swimming fifteen laps in an Olympic pool every morning is very easy for a gold medalist.

Methods

I. <u>Keep a diary.</u> This helps you extract your development from the chaos and trivia of your life. It is a sacred text, if kept honestly. Here is how you begin.

A. Write a description of what you want to achieve. This should describe your material goals, your career goals, your magical goals, the Initiatory virtues you wish to possess, and the type of person you want to be.

B. Make a list of all of your good qualities. Label it "Innate Patterns to Develop More Fully."

C. Make a list of all of your bad qualities and habits. Be absolutely brutal with yourself! Label it "Hindrances to my Power."

At least four days a week make an entry in your diary. Write anything you want from your fears and failures to your brightest triumphs, but include four things in each entry.

1. Something you did to further your goals
2. Your best thought or breakthrough
3. Something you did to get rid of, weaken, or modify a bad habit
4. Something you plan to do in the immediate future to further your goals

You should also write down all the magical operations that you do, as well as any results that you note from them. Likewise particularly vivid dreams and meaningful synchronicities should go on the list.

Bad habits can be ended in three ways. First simply stop them (easy to say, hard to do). Second **consciously** pit them against each other. Let's say your bad habits include procrastination and nonproductive anger. Well the next time you feel that you are about to throw a fit, tell yourself, "I know that I should be mad at Bob, but I'll do it tomorrow." If you succeed in your weakness matching, make a note of the Victory. Third bad habits can be knocked out of the way with good behavior. Let's say your bad habit is watching a half hour of TV you don't like, between two shows you do enjoy. Well fill up that time with your diary work, and note it as a Victory.

II. <u>Learn to care for and train your body.</u> This has seven parts.

A. Give up auto-poisoning activity. Addictions must die; magicians control the world, and are not controlled by it.

B. Learn to eat right, exercise, and get adequate sleep.

C. Learn the family weaknesses so that you can avoid them.

D. Learn your likely date of death, so that you can plan to have done what you want to do in the world by them.

E. Begin a training program for the body that gives you control over it. The best programs for this are martial arts that teach both grace and practical self defense.

F. Meditate on the Chemistry of life in your plans and dealings with others. What kind of things can you do in your 20s (like all-night shamanic vigils) that you won't do in your 50s? Learn how to make the stages of life work with your goals. See how successful people around you do this. See how it could make successful those you wish to empower.

G. Explore your sexuality. Don't assume that anyone's model of you is right; assume that you don't yet know the correct way to worship yourself.

III. <u>Master a traditional system of magic.</u> I can't stress this enough. Most postmodern Left Hand Path movements suggest that a magician should create his or her own (as do I), but they don't tell you to find something to test yourself against. Of course you can master a system *you* come up with! There are five aspects to mastering a system.

A. Memory training. Can you learn to keep a set of ideas clearly in your mind, so that you can use them for tools?

B. Practice in specific techniques such as body posture, visualization, vocalic skills, learning to make incenses and perfumes.

C. Checking at how good you are against the experience of others. Can you get the results that others have received in the past?

D. Learning how to universalize your knowledge and experience. After you have undergone training, can you then extract the principles and use them in your life? For example if you learn about the Runes, can you speak and think clearly about the concept of Mystery? If you learn Hermetics, can you talk clearly about how Plato's model — that the philosopher has power in the world — is related to the notion of *As above, so below*?

E. Teaching the system. Can you learn the system so that you can teach it? This not only proves your skill in the system, but can earn you both money (on the physical plane) and skill at teaching, which will serve you at later phases of your Initiation.

When looking for a traditional system, don't choose something that is the product of one man or woman. Look for something that has worked in the world for some time. Look for a system that has some scholarly literature available on it, as well practical "how-to" stuff.

To understand what makes up a traditional system, a thorough reading of the many works of Mircea Eliade is recommended.

Pick a system that is Resonant with your self. If you are a wild man, biker dude, don't learn about the Golden Dawn. If your favorite magical chamber is your library with a roaring fire beside you, don't investigate shamanism.

IV. <u>Create you own System of magic.</u> All your life you have had certain things that have worked your soul. They are yours and yours alone. For example some of your main magical influences could have been the television series *Dark Shadows*, hearing a ghost story at summer camp, and then discovering that your great grand uncle Nathaniel was in some peculiar Nineteenth Century magical order. Take from these things what you need to create your own rituals, meditations, and practices. See what works and what doesn't. Let practicality and fun be your twin guides. Over the years many things will enter in and leave your personal system. Just keep three things in mind:

A. Never reveal all your secrets to others, anymore than you tell them your ATM number. There is a great power in personal things.

B. After you have assembled your personal system, write it up in your diary. Then read an introductory book on anthropology. Go back and look at your system. What does it tell you about your values, trends, strengths, and weaknesses? Personal choice reveals aspects of the core self. Often in the most playful and free moments the core self acts directly on the surface.

C. Some of your personal methods can be passed on as Gifts to people that you want to empower. This is a very precious and intimate Gift, give it wisely. Be very honored if you should receive such a Gift. Keep these things out of the books you write and the lectures you give, but be sure to Give to others what was Given to you; this is one of the ways that Mouth-to-Ear Initiation lives on in this planet.

V. <u>Write a Magical Autobiography.</u> We seldom realize how rich our life has been; we never realize our blind spots. There are two times to write a magical autobiography. This first is early in your magical career and it is called the Book of Freedom. The second comes in midcareer and is called the Book of Secrets. After both have been written, you will know enough about your coming into Being that you can revise this list of 19 practices for the rest of your earthly incarnation. If you have by that time become a Teacher, the new list will be helpful for your school, which should maintain a cordial relationship (or perhaps belong to the framework of) the School where your eyes were Opened.

A. The Book of Freedom. This practice is similar to the *Recapitulation* in the magical system of Carlos Castaneda, or the making of amends in various 12-step programs. It involves a deeply critical look at one's effect on others, so that you may pay off your debts to them. Now this is not done for reasons of karma or of celestial justice. The Left Hand Path Initiate knows that there is no justice in the world, save what he or she causes to come here. This practice is connected with what is esoterically known as the Pergamon Principle— that the effect the Initiate has on the earth is based on the sum total of his effects on the earth. So the Initiate wants to end any bad or stupid things he did. To create the Book of Freedom, there is a three-step process.

1. Make a list of all the bad things in your life. Bad things done to you, and more importantly, bad things you did to others.

2. Picture the bad events. Play them over and over in the movie theater of your mind. Each time let the hurt grow less, the anger grow less, and imagine yourself breathing out the bad energy that others have directed to you, and breathing in your own energy (good or bad) that you directed to others. Do this until you can view the worst scenes of your life neutrally.

3. Do what rational things you can to make amends for your past actions. If the victims of your past actions are no longer incarnated, stand alone on a starry night and simply say your apologies aloud to them.

When this process is done (and it can take months or years) you will have a strong sense of Freedom. You will have regained lost energies. Your health will have improved, and you will have developed self-honesty.

B. The Book of Secrets. This should be done after you are deeply on your path, say ten years after reading this book. Write a history of your life beginning with the mysterious event that brought your grandparents together, and going through all the strange and beautiful twists and turns of your life. After you have written it, put it aside for awhile. Then read it to discover hidden things about yourself. What are you on Earth for? What gets better in your presence? What things have really Opened Doors for you? You will then have hard data to plan the rest of your life with.

C. Revise this list. Sometime after you have gone through the two-part process above, you will be able to come up with a much finer-tuned set of practices than these, and should both enact and teach them.

VI. <u>Practice Self Sufficiency.</u> Because of the attitude of Dependence forced upon us by corporations and the government, we often think we can do nothing. We must buy every service, wait for permission for every action, and otherwise pay for our right to pay some more. Learn how to do as many things as you can for yourself. Grow your own garden, work out your troubles with your neighbors, lead a neighborhood watch group, learn to shop away from the mall, pick your own fashions rather than having fashion dictated to you. In an age of Dependency, the antinomian action is independence.

VII. <u>Learn Admiration.</u> It is easy to see the many flaws of the world and mankind. If that is all you look at, you will feel yourself far superior to your true state. Learn to see the heroism in the lives of people that you encounter, learn to see the magic in the world nearest you, learn to see the beauty in the world. Perception is a willed act, and it determines the world you live in. There are forces, mainly commercial, that have a vested interest in you seeing the ugliness and danger of the world versus the prepackaged beauty and safety they would sell you. Fight against this.

VII. <u>Do a yearly inventory.</u> Every year there's a vast conspiracy called the Christmas-New Years season. It is filled with people driven by angst and guilt buying presents for people they fear or have mistreated or neglected. These same people spend the season getting drunk so they don't have to face the agony of their failures, or the misery of having to plan for next year. Go out among them one night. Look at them, and what drives them. The next night, find a quiet happy place where you can see how your Work of separating yourself from them is going. Be both brutal with inventory and excited by the prospects of the next year.

• Assess your overall state as of this time last year. Are you where you want to be magically, spiritually, financially? Is your health strong? Your love-life desirable? Your mind filled with new knowledge, your life with new skills? Have you overcome your shortcomings? Have you found your greatest weakness and begun war against its outer manifestation? Forgive yourself your failures, rejoice in your accomplishments, and above all plan on how to make next year better.

• Bury the hatchet. Left Hand Path Initiates need not forgive their enemies, but hatred takes a lot of valuable force. Look over your enemies list, and forgive those folk who need not have such energy directed against them. Like unplugging a lot of needless appliances, you'll have a great deal more energy when the process is done. Take the same time to cull your life of false friends and psychic vampires that are likewise drains on your life. We often forget that these little lampreys have attached themselves to our chests over the year, and that they need pruning just as unnecessary hatred does.

• Curse your real enemies. Look over the year. If you do have people who are really and truly threatening you, your family, your School let that energy fly before New Year's Day. Look over the year. If you find that certain people have been a great help to your Initiation, send them your magical blessings. This isn't altruism, this is paying back, which is a Left Hand Path virtue.

• Look over your life for the path of your magical unfolding. Think about what really has awakened you. Look for the patterns in your life. Finding those patterns is finding your true will. Learn how the Will feels, and resolve to let it have more of a voice in planning next year.

• Write down the results of your inventory; you may need to revise your good and bad trait list in your diary.

A. A sample Blessing. Light a red candle. Think of the person who has helped you, let Love well up within you, and then say these words,

"Oh (Name of Person) I Speak and the guards of the treasure house of the World rush to bring you the fine things you deserve. O (Name of Person) I Will and the force of vitality blooms in your body. Oh (Name of

Person) I Enchant and all look upon you with adoring eyes and open minds. Oh (Name of Person) I Conjure and your luck grows great in all things. Oh (Name of Person) I Invoke and the Lore you Need will find its way to you. Oh (Name of Person) I Bewitch and your enemies fall into a year-long sleep. Oh (Name of Person) I Charm and lost friends and stolen goods are returned you even from the ends of the Earth. Oh (Name of Person) I Bind all things which stand against you within and without, so that you may go far! Oh (Name of Person) I Loose all things that may come to you to Teach, Bless, and Enrich! I who am the Elder Magician, whose Sorcery is a thing of legend among the gods, cause the waters of the briny sea to give you their pearls, I cause the flames of the mighty forges to fashion your adornments, I cause the black roses of the night to sweeten your air, I cause the dark loam of the forest to cushion your step. My friend, the Prince of Darkness, joins his Will with mine in these words, that you have Awareness, Health, Joy, and Riches! I will stand by you as you have stood by me, and my magic will fetch others from the ends of the earth to stand with you as well!"

B. A Sample Curse. Light a black candle. Write the name of the person you wish to curse on a slip of paper in green ink, write other things like their titles, nicknames, their name of genealogy (as in son of Roger). Say the words and burn the slip.

"As a fit ruling power of the Earth I end the effectiveness of (Name of Person) in all things. They are hollow and resent those who burn with Purpose. I make their lives as hollow as they. Oh (Name of Person) I Speak and shut off all crossroads to you. Oh (Name of Person) I Bewitch you and fill your mind with confusion. Oh (Name of Person) I Reveal you, and all of your friends and family shall see you as you truly are. Oh (Name of Person) I Condemn you and all demons, ghosts of those who died before their hour, all spells loosed upon the world shall haunt you day and night. Oh (Name of Person) I Invoke and your name is on the malicious gossip's tongue. Oh (Name of Person) I Hex you and cause the poisons and sicknesses in your body to weaken and weary you. Oh (Name of Person) I Curse you with all manner of ill luck. Oh (Name of Person) I Bind to thee all hurtful things that have plagued my friends and family. They fly to you! Oh (Name of Person) I Loose all things that would seek you out to do harm to you. I, who am the Malicious One, whose Sorcery is feared by the gods, cause the sea to vomit forth monsters to tear at your flesh. I cause the flames of destruction to burn away all that you have wrought. I cause tornadoes to blow away your name and memory. I cause the stones of the Earth to wound your feet in your endless, loveless, tormented wanderings. My friend, the Prince of Darkness, joins his Will to mine that you will have Sorrow, Shame, and Sickness! I will be wary that you do not hurt me, and my magic fetches thousands to hurt you as you hurt me, even if they must be brought from the ends of the earth!"

VIII. <u>Discover your Roots.</u> Your physical inheritance is your biggest and best tool for self development. The need to know yourself, your limits, and your possible skills begins with knowing your body. There is a great deal of magical information encoded in your blood. In the Left Hand Path we realize that one race is not the superior of another race, and that policy which comes from such favoritism is a form of Right Hand Path practice where the concept of the "Folk" comes to replace the concept of "God." We also realize that every human is a walking product of millions of years of human striving, and that his or her genes have been influenced by thousands of years of magical practice. It would be sheer folly not to discover what magical treasures you may already possess because of your physical inheritance. This reflects the Left Hand Path maxim, "It is hard work to mine gold, but you get better results in a gold mine." I will give an example of an American male of mainly Greek descent discovering his magical roots. The levels are arbitrary — going to "F" is further then most people will have the skill, will, or time to do.

A. First year. Steals a blessed wafer from a Greek Orthodox Church, and performs a Black Mass of his own devising (perhaps using Anton La Vey's "Homage to Tchort" as a base text), takes modern Greek classes at a local college, has the word ALETHEIA tattooed over his heart, begins to make amends with all of his blood relatives. Reads Homer in translation. Reads *The Early Greek Concept of the Soul* by Jan Bremmer. These actions break the individual free from existing belief systems, magically announces his desire to Uncover things (ALETHEIA), gives him contact with tradition (language classes and Homer), and gives him some notion of the soulcraft of his people (making amends plus the Bremmer book).

B. Second year. Obtain *Hermetic Magic* by Stephen E. Flowers. Study it and perform the magical rituals in it until you achieve results. Read the books of Carl Kerenyi, especially his *Hermes* and *Prometheus*. Join a Greek heritage society. The awakened soul begins to use magical techniques, and the outer life begins to explore possibilities for action in the world.

C. Third year. Read Erwin Rhode's *Psyche: The Cult of Souls and Belief in Immorality Among the Greeks*. Begin classical Greek studies. Sign up for such Internet lists that discuss topics of interest to you such as Plato-L. Begin asking for source material on Greek religion and magic. (This introduces you to the scholarly community after you are of enough substance to ask interesting questions.)

D. Fourth year. Begin writing magical diary in Greek. Read a good translation of Plato's *The Republic* (such as the G. M. A. Grube translation) and a good commentary on it (such as C. D. C. Reeve's *Philosopher-Kings: the Argument of Plato's Republic.*) This introduces you to Sovereignty in cultural context, and begins your awakening on a personal level.)

E. Fifth year. Travel to Greece. Visit magical sites to perform your magical work, meet distant cousins.

F. The above will have opened many, many avenues for exploration: follow them, and eventually write a good book on Greek magic. Have it published in English and Greek.

IX. Discover your location. Another great Tool in deciding what kind of Work to do on yourself is knowing where you are. As humans we seldom are Awake enough to know anything, and therefore we lose out on a Great Truth of the Left Hand Path. The Truth is "If you have the potential to be a god, you will have all you need right in front of you." Learning to use where you are, whether it is a small town in Kansas, the middle of Manhattan, or a tree house in the African veldt, is part of the Initiatory job. Here are some things to do.

A. Obtain a map of your area. Systematically explore it, street by street. Use each exploration to remind yourself that you Sleep through too many things. Make a list of all the possible resources you see. Use these things to amuse and empower you. One of the ways mankind lulls itself to sleep is by tribalism. The people that go to Goth clubs might not go to pancake dinners at a nearby church, the folks that frequent the great foreign film series on campus might not shop the bargains at the railroad salvage store. You know no such barriers. All of your region is a magical labyrinth for your benefit. Remember this and practice it.

B. Become interested in local politics. Here more than anywhere else you will discover the difference between what people say, and what they want. Local politics are a lab in learning the true motivations for things. You will find greed and corruption worse than you thought humans were capable of, and you will find nobility and strengths as well. As you learn to look for what is really going on, your political opinions will seem all over the map to your friends. This too will teach you some things about the social construction of reality.

C. Learn about the magical lore of your region. Some places (like the Isle of Man) are so deeply magical that it would almost be harder not to know. Other places may take a good deal of research to discover anything. But anywhere man has been, magic has been, and its effects remain. After you gain your lore, not only can you impress your friends and guests, but you can try to make magical contact with the currents of your area. This lets you tap into what is already Working on yourself and your fellow citizens, but it also lets your effect the future with your Essence.

X. Join a School. This is a Necessity at a certain level of development. In the beginning all of our breakthroughs come to us when we are alone. All beginning meaningful steps of evolution are begun while one is alone. But the time comes when you will need to see certain objective manifestations of what you suspect to be true. Many occultists avoid this, because of fear of personal inadequacy. But you come to realize that "Gee even if I'm the smallest potato there, at least I can learn more."

Schools help you extract knowledge that you already have. But Schools provide a dilemma for the Left Hand Path Initiate— he or she must submit voluntarily to the school. This requires superhuman effort. Let me explain.

If you are in a structure that you must do the work or else, the work requires a semi-human effort (say working in fast food). If you are in an environment where if you do the work you get certain rewards, the work requires a human effort (say most corporate jobs). If you volunteer for a place of hard work so that you will be transformed, the work requires an heroic effort (say volunteering for the Marines— you volunteered, but after you're there you're getting up at 4:40 in the morning on a nonvoluntary basis). If you volunteer to be in a place where the work is suggested but not enforced, doing the work requires a superhuman effort (say the Temple of Set).

In a School, you won't get far if the only job is grunt work. You won't get far if the only job is "play." But if passage through the School requires that you self-motivate to use the formulas they give you, you can go very far indeed if you don't fall into the all-too-human games of politics, but strive at the Greater-than-Human game which comprises the Left Hand Path.

XI. Learn to Sing and Tell Jokes. Most Left Hand Path Initiates have a great deal of character armor that the shocks of their lives have caused them to build. This use of psychic force as a buffer against the world ceases to be necessary once the Initiate learns to trust him- or herself. If it is not dismantled, it will keep magic from flowing out into the world for sorcery, and will not allow outside forces to be drawn in the Sovereign self. One of the best ways to achieve this needed flow is to get over the vast weight of self importance that most of us carry around. Uncle Setnakt recommends two methods:

A. Learn to sing. Singing is a great reliever of stress, it charms and disarms many people, and is a great medium for many magical systems. People that can sing in front of other people lose their crippling shyness, they learn how to control people by voice alone (try leading a chorus, you'll see what I mean), and they learn how to overcome stresses at will— you can't sing if your chest is tight.

B. Learn to tell jokes. Having a sense of humor is a necessity for intelligent persons regardless of their spiritual path (or lack of one). Otherwise the tensions of the world would make them go nuts. Humor is an attempt to remind ourselves of the Chaotic nature of the world. It actually represents a moment of Platonic Memory (αναμνησις), and is a foretaste of part of our divine nature. So from a Left Hand Path viewpoint, humor is one of the ways of knowing our Possibilities. Being able to be funny is a partially learned skill that should be honed. It will give you four advantages. One, it gains the friendship of some and deflects the anger of other intelligent people. Two, it will Teach you Timing, which is the most important lesson for magical operations. Three, it allows for speculation and playfulness, which are expressions of the Initiatory virtue of Openness. Four, it lets people talk to you, because it puts them at ease.

XII. Learn Philosophy. The Greeks bequeathed a great gift to mankind. They were able to talk about very uncommon things like Justice, Truth, and Beauty. Their system of speech was not encoded in rituals and knowledge of their pantheon, but in a clear and simple method of discourse. Thus we can pick up their work millennia later and be moved and instructed thereby. If we look at most other cultures such as Egypt or ancient Mexico, we have to learn the pantheon, we have to know the rituals, and slowly we can read what is encoded in the myths— taking much more of ourselves into the interpretation than in the method of philosophy.

The Left Hand Path initiate studies philosophy so that he or she can articulate (both for him- or herself as well as for others) what he or she knows and what he or she holds True, and by what standards. Philosophy is the best tool for acquiring Meaning. It is not enough to simply read the great philosophical texts, one must discuss them and write on them. The first step is a college-level Introduction to Philosophy course. The second step is acquiring people who will talk about these matters with you.

In addition to a good understanding of the outlines of philosophy, the Left Hand Path initiate should possess a good understanding of logic— methods of induction and deduction, the basic questions of epistemology, ontology, ethics, and metaphysics. Some particularly helpful thinkers for the Left Hand Path are Plato, Husserl, Whitehead (Process philosophy is *very* useful to the LHP Initiate), Nietzsche, Wittgenstein, Peirce, and Bergson. You needn't buy the collected works of these fellows, but dip deeply into each, and let your inclination take you further. Like all the other activities on this list, this is a lifelong affair.

Only when you can express your own ideas without reference to magical systems and exotic words, can you be said to have mastered the Path.

XIII. Learn a psychological system. The major thing that the Left Hand Path Initiate seeks to change is the way his mind-body complex acts. It is useful to have access to the many, many things we know about the mind, and to gain insight into its works. This means that one should have first an understanding of the popular literature on mental studies, and a college-level Introduction to Psychology course, so that you will recognize how memory works, and the way humans develop. This is learning about the clay you are going to work with. Secondly one should look into a non-mystical psychological system that emphasizes positive self change as a possibility. One should avoid systems that teach a "victim mentality." Here's an example. In a victim system you might learn/discover that all your problems stem from the way your parents treated you, and so it is understandable that you are a failure. In a self-change system you might learn that you hold your parents responsible for your failures, and it is your job to change that attitude.

Two excellent systems for the Left Hand Path Initiate to learn about are the optimal psychology of Mihaly Csikszentmihalyi and the psychosynthesis of Roberto Assagioli.

Learning about psychology has four benefits. Firstly, and most importantly it can teach you to be gentle with yourself. Secondly, it explains why change takes time. Thirdly, is gives you a language that allows you to talk about your change processes with your friends and

41

colleagues without the use of magical or mystical terms. Fourthly, if you (or someone you love) should need the attention of a mental health practitioner, this helps you make informed choices.

Some immature forms of the LHP hold the notion of therapy in disregard. Mature LHP systems stress that knowing what help you need, and getting it, is a virtue. Do not conceal your magical or Initiatory practices from your therapist, merely be careful in choosing a therapist who will respect your belief system and your privacy. Giving them a copy of this book is not a bad idea (and is helpful to Uncle Setnakt's pocketbook).

XIV. <u>Do the Grand Initiation</u>. After you have had success with your sorcery and done a few of the items on this list — you may of course have done several of them before you even heard of this book — you should do the Grand Initiation. It is very hard to do. It will benefit you at any level of Initiation you possess, and in any truly Left Hand Path School you belong to. Most of the people buying this book will find it too difficult to do, and will not truly profit by holding this volume. The Grand Initiation *activates* all the ideas in the book within your psyche.

XV. <u>Plan for your retirement</u>. Since the Left Hand Path stresses play and self-love, there is an overabundance of hedonism in it. This is as it should be: if you are going to have too much of anything, it should be self love, because that can be changed into a desire to work on one's self fairly easily. Unfortunately, overreliance on magic and too much hedonism make for very broke old people. The Left Hand Path Initiate spends as much time at Estate Planning Seminars as they do going through that Fire-Walking Course. Left Hand Path Initiates save up for their retirement for four reasons. Firstly, it ties every magical act now into a sense of the whole life. My sorcery that gets me a job when I'm twenty, gives me a little something when I'm eighty. This is great training for immortality. Secondly, it puts forth the magical wish that your whole life will be spent collecting the wisdom of the world, so that when you retire you will create the great crystallization of your Work. If in your heart you know that the LHP is only something that you're going to be involved in for four years and then you'll have a garage sale, you aren't really an Initiate. Thirdly, it reminds you to carefully pick friends and allies that you will want to be around forty years from now. This teaches you to control your temper and to be loyal. Fourthly, it will provide you with certain things to place in the world to continue your will after your death. This could be anything from a scholarship at a local college in your name, to giving a great collection of magical jewelry to your students. This type of link will aid your interactions with the material universe after you are gone.

XVI. <u>Practice an art</u>. Play an instrument, sculpt, write poetry, land-scape— something! In artistic creation a moment comes when the artists feel as though they are at one with their instrument and the work of art they are creating. This is not a union with the universe, it is the moment that you are actually acting on the universe without the opinion of yourself that is part of your medial level being in the way. This feeling is a direct experience of godhood. The art so produced may be good or bad according to your talent and training, but it will produce a strong magical effect to further your Initiation. This type of *flow* experience is well described by Csikszentmihalyi, and his books are good gateways for the artist-magician. Nietzsche described it as well, "In their creativity, artists express the proper relationship to the world. They express the will-to-power. They are self-creating in their activity and in this sense they take power over the world."

XVII. <u>Master the Internet and the World Wide Web</u>. Now the key word here is "Master." The Internet and the World Wide Web are manifestations of the medial level of the world, which means that they are neutral energies that can work as much against you as for you. As the Internet grows to be more and more of the nervous system of the world, it will come more and more to be the great connector to the medial level of activity. If you are interested in knowing when this will happen, try web-searches on the "Extropians" and the "Singularity."

To master the WWW, you have to develop a strong bullshit detector, and a strong sense of what makes up good scholarship as opposed to baseless speculation. If you do this, you will have the treasures of the world's libraries no matter where you live.

To master the Internet, you have to learn to control your own medial level. You need to wean yourself of the constant need for strokes, or the constant need to vent anger at morons. If you can learn to use the Internet as a way of connecting and interacting with smart people with similar interests, you can do anything given time and determination of your associates.

Consider this, the Knights Templar began as just nine people— but nine smart people with good connections. Not only did they become the method of transmission of Sufi wisdom to the West, and the mythic model of many fraternities— after they were banned in France, they continued on in Portugal as the Order of Christ, under which name their Grandmaster Henry the Navigator mapped a great deal of the world. Determination, enlightened self-sacrifice, networking have always had the power to change the world. The levels of determination and enlightened self-sacrifice are low in the world (but can be made high in the Initiate of the Left Hand Path by practice) but the ability to network is at an all-time high.

XVIII. <u>Go on Pilgrimages</u>. The Initiate of the Left Hand Path has the lifetime duty not only of entertaining and enchanting him- or herself, but also of realizing that his or her Essence is not of this world. We work better upon the galling limitations of time and space, when we know that we are in part and potential not wholly native to the mechanistic cosmos. One of the best ways to remind ourselves of this is travel. We put ourselves in different places, and see the things that our fellow humans only dream of seeing. If you have always wanted to go to Stonehenge or the Temple at Luxor— do so! The whole process of the trip — from planning to working magic to get the funds for the trip there and back — will change you in subtle ways. Likewise learning to make entirely personal pilgrimages, like trips to your hometown to see how you and it have changed since you left, are a sacred form of Play for the Left Hand Path Initiate.

XIX. Stand up for the Path. There is a basic magical principle, that if you want your magic to work, you have to affirm it. This is especially true of the Left Hand Path, affirming it is always an act of antinomianism that helps break the fetters that bind you to the herd mentality. Standing up for the path also lets you Create it, and Teach it. Learning how to do this will bring you a score of other skills. Be wise and speak from places of safety. It might mean writing a newspaper to correct the myths of "satanic activity." It might mean getting better books in your local library. It might mean sticking up for unpopular religious causes. It might mean getting local bookstores to carry this book. It might mean shutting down a group that calls itself LHP, but is in reality a license to criminality. All of these things further Awareness, Teach how to deal with people, and by their commission strengthen the activity of the Prince of Darkness on this world.

Now this is a very hard list. If you were expecting an easy list of activities in a book on how to become a Superman, you were a fool. But these nineteen gates to the Left Hand Path (as it exists now) have certain principles lying behind them— the soft mastery of which comes from the hard mastery of them. These principles are easy to discuss, but can only be Understood experientially.

The Guiding Principles Behind LHP Initiation
The guiding principles behind these practices are Trust, Honesty, Forgiveness, Growth, Artistry, and Extraction. Let's look at each of these principles.
Trust. The Initiate must develop Trust in him- or herself. In traditional religious and spiritual disciplines, a higher-level Initiate shows an example of magical power, and the newer Initiate begins out of desire for what the other has, and a sense of self worthlessness since they couldn't do the miracle. In the Left Hand Path, it is necessary to experience your own miracles first, so that you can Trust that you have powers and potentials that simply aren't at your command. Your desire to have these things at your command will pull you along the Path, and the fact that sometimes you have such abilities and sometimes not will Teach you a great lesson: that you are as Mysterious as anything else in the Cosmos. Once that sense of Trust is developed, two other things may happen. One, you will begin to develop a sense of daring that lets you put yourself in novel situations, and you will come to see the truth of the maxim that Fortune Favors the Bold. Two, you will be able to meet with extraordinary men and women,

44

and not be cowed into submission by their abilities, but be moved by an honest (and humbling) admiration that a beginning skier might feel for an Olympic-class skier.

Honesty. The Initiate will learn that he has been telling him- or herself a large number of lies all his or her life. Some of these lies are exaggerations of positive attributes, others are negative slanders, and many are statements of certainty in areas where nothing certain can be said. The overriding Truth is that these lies are not only inaccurate, but incoherent. They don't give a unified picture of the Self: you may tell your mother that you are a good artist, you may tell yourself that you suck, and you may tell your best friend that art doesn't matter to you. The Initiate learns that telling himself the Truth is the only way to start to change himself, and that means asking himself tough questions, being fair with himself, and not rushing to make statements on things that all the facts aren't in on yet. This principle is very hard to work with, because of its apparent simplicity.

Forgiveness. Many people "get into" magic because of a kind of self-loathing. They are attracted to the Dark, not because of its Mystery, but because they feel that they are unworthy of the Light. "Magic" and "Initiation" become great excuses to beat themselves up. When they fail at the hard job of doing magic, which is the most difficult art for human beings to master (even now when the world is at its loosest), they can indulge in feeling really bad about themselves. True Initiates know they will fail. They'll stop keeping their diaries, they'll not do the knowledge-gathering task, they will fall asleep from time to time. This must be accepted. The only important thing is that as soon as you can, get back on the path. Develop for yourself a forgiveness of past mistakes. You should have the unconditional love of a mother for your past, and the unconditional harshness of a drill sergeant when meeting the present to Become a Sovereign in the future.

Growth. The activities listed above for the most part have the idea of increasing pressure built up in them. You will not get far in some of the activities, others will truly open Doors for you, and as each Door is opened the challenges must be made to increase. True self change occurs by upping the ante each month, each year, each decade. To have the time to do this requires you take control of more and more of your life. You will even find that certain types of cognition will become available to you during sleep. These changes are for the most part very small, but their cumulative effect is enormous. It is the nature of the Path that you do not reach your goal, but merely have increasing images of it delivered to you. If you learn to accept this, the Path will provide for you rewards beyond your wildest dreams.

Artistry. The above list seems pretty daunting. How can anyone accomplish so much? The answer is in combining your goals in an artistic fashion. For example, let's say you are an Italian American. You take a boat trip to Italy. On the way you study the works of Benedetto Croce, one of the most profound philosophers on the relation between human consciousness and history, in the original Italian. You make sketches of

45

your fellow passengers— you work on deck during the day, seduce your fellow travelers at night, and make connections with local scholars that can take you to certain ruins associated with the obscure Roman demoness Meftis, one of the greatest Initiators into the Daemonic Realms, and you are able to tell the scholar that she is not alone, that there are others following the *via sinistra* (and thus open a Door for the Left Hand Path in Cremona in the early twenty-first century just as it had flourished there in the first). You of course keep all this in your journal, and when you return a decade later, you re-read it as a way of studying your process— as well as that of your lovely and brainy friend, the witch of Cremona. This blending of many gateways makes one into a true disciple of the Black Arts.

Extraction. The practice of the Left Hand Path is one of extracting the essences and structures of phenomena within and beyond one's self and working directly upon them. This will-to-knowledge evolves in many areas, but slowly pervades the whole of the Initiate's life. At first she learns to see that what she has been taught, or what she has been led to believe, isn't true. Then she learns to use her powers of reason and observation to discover what is true. Eventually (but rarely) she will even come to have direct knowledge of things. It will be as though she has developed subtle organs that hear what is thought, rather than what is said; that will see where things are going, rather than where they rest; that will feel the true weight of events, rather than be misled by the world's scales. This process will not only give the Initiate Power and Knowledge, but will give them Speed and Timing as well, as they come to extract the real wherever they are and whatever they are doing.

Chapter Three

The Grand Initiation

This rite should only be done after this book has been read through a few times, and success has been gained at some of the practices mentioned in the last chapter. If you are new to magical practice, it is strongly suggested that you have some successes at sorcery and divination before beginning a Rite of this magnitude.

The Rite will benefit anyone of any level of Initiation in the Left Hand Path.

Performance of this rite will open possibilities in you for self change and world change that have lain latent since before your birth. It will bring you luck and lore and opportunities at the right time for the rest of your life. The rite consists of an entry rite and nine sets of nine nights.

The following things apply throughout. *You must keep a diary of just this rite*, beginning on the first day of the Chaos section, and ending the night before the last day of the Victory section. You will make at least four regular entries during each nine-day section and one Letterist entry (see below). You must make an entry after each of the rites, except for the sixth section, which has its own rules. The diary must have black covers.

During the rite you need to *observe the following rules*. In addition to reading the material for the section, you should read other material or watch films pertaining to the topic of the nine nights. You must otherwise cut down your media intake as much as possible. You must not drink or take any form of recreational drugs during the work. You must speak as little as possible about performing the Rite as you can. If you can keep it a total Secret, so much the better.

You must avoid all other magical practice. No sorcery, no divination, no group rites, no religious observances. You must remove all magical jewelry you own. You must not use any magical tool that has been consecrated to any other purpose than this rite.

You must observe the Rule of the New. If any opportunity comes your way during the session, you must take it if it is out of your ordinary routine. If your fellow employees want to go bowling, and you would normally never think of going bowling, then you must bowl.

You must say the Day-Taking rite each morning (as described in the first section), *and the Night-Taking rite each night.*

You must engage in the following visualization frequently. As you stand or walk or sit, become aware of the bigness of the planet beneath you. Think of great black streams rushing up from the depths of the Earth, from along the surface, from the sky above. They converge in you, and as they flow through you, you feel that you are storing up their energy. As they pass into you streams of yellow and green pus pass out of you— these are your weaknesses, sicknesses, and bad habits passing away.

Letterism. Each nine-day period has a letter assigned to it. For one of your diary entries, instead of engaging in the meditations suggested, draw the letter and draw a circle around it. Underneath write everything that comes to mind looking at the letter. For example the letter for the third week is "L". Here is a start of what you might write (notice that it is very free form):

Life, and Lust and Love all things I long for, Lamed begins Leviathan, Laguz is life and luck, I see eleven lavender loons flying over an L-shaped lake, evil is live spelled backwards, late, I love lilies and lilacs and leopards and leopard-lovers, the message of Initiation is that it is always later than you think, luck, how much is controlled by magic, lock, real magic is either knowing how to put more locks on things or how to unlock things, what if I want it unlocked and another magician wants to lock it, what should be locked away, loose, Uncle Setnakt says the world is loose now, so that one can obtain in one lifetime, does that mean it used to take more than one lifetime?

And so forth, spend as long on this free association as you do on the regular entries, which should take from fifteen minutes to half an hour.

Your magical chamber should have an altar that you can write at, a glass to drink from, some candles, an incense burner to burn an incense that suggests magic to you (you'll want to try out a few types before this rite); it should have a hand mirror; it should be a place where you will not be interrupted during the performance of the rites, or when you are writing in your diary.

The rite should be performed so that shortly after its ending, a significant life change is about to occur. Good times are before starting graduate school, before beginning an around-the-world tour, joining the military, starting a new business, having a significant birthday. Otherwise days important to the Left Hand Path's immediate future may be used such as May 5, 2000; April 30, 2001; or December 21, 2012.

The Opening Rite

Preparations. You will have purchased a complete suit of new clothes from underwear to outer wear to put on the next day. You will have a place to put your old clothes. You will have made a paper chain with six lengths, you will have gathered some symbolic item that relates to old belief systems (for example if you were a Christian, the Bible; a Scientologist, *Dianetics*; a Muslim, the *Koran*; an atheist, *Free Thought Today*; and so forth), you will gather certain symbolic objects that refer to past dependencies (such as food stamps, an alcohol bottle, a credit card you maxed-out, a picture of your parents' home that you lived in too many years as an adult, or a crack rock). Prepare your magical chamber as in general instructions above. You will need a small table as a secondary altar, with a sliced red apple on it, as well as the symbolic items and the method of their destruction.

Dress in your favorite clothes; you will put them away after the rite and not wear them again until the Grand Initiation's conclusion.

Opening: Hiss like a serpent for some seconds, until the sibilant sound begins to relax you. Speak the words in quotation marks.

"The sky is held up by four pillars."

48

Picture a black pillar to the left of you and a white pillar to the right.

"To my left is the Desire for Power in matter. Here is my longing for Wealth, for Love, for Fame, for Followers. Seeking these Shadowed things will bring me great change. Hail the Power that seeks only to do Evil, but achieves only the Good!

"To my right is the Desire for Quality in Mind. Here is my longing for Beauty, Justice, Truth, and endless Creativity. Glimpses of these fleeting things will drive me to great quests. Hail the Graal which brings dissatisfaction to the world!"

"Behind me is a life richer than I have realized, whose Mysteries Shape me in accordance with my Will, and the Will of others who have Worked before me, and the Will of the Prince of Darkness Himself!

"Before me is the Darkness of the Unmanifest, mysterious land of ultimate Freedom, where I will die and be reborn as I Become a suitable companion for the Prince of Darkness!"

Advance to the small table. Pick up the hand mirror.

"I forgive myself of all my past failures, for I have no more time for guilt. I give myself the Sight to see the locked Doors within myself, and the Courage to open them at the right time, knowing that I must Know myself. I give myself the Hearing to listen to my better judgment, and the Trust to act upon it. I give myself the sense of Touch that I may know the Treasures that I have in my life, but have been lost to."

Pick up the apple slices and eat them slowly. They will give you the Gifts you have spoken of.

Place your left hand on your temple.

"My Mind has absorbed Setnakt's Book, and it yearns to be free."

Place your left hand on your heart.

"My Heart has longed to be as a god since my earliest memory."

Place your left hand on your navel.

"My Will has been Touched by the Essence of the Prince of Darkness and it has Awakened."

Place your left hand on your genitals.

"My Body courses with excitement. It is the Bull that god rides. It is a great snarling beast whose senses now come alive for the purpose of the Great Work.

"My body, my will, my heart, and my mind are in harmony. Old time stops, and a new creation begins."

Look at the objects of past belief systems. Say the following words and destroy them in whatever manner is emotionally satisfying. Feel free to add more words if so moved.

"Fetters from my previous life, you pulled me apart, chaining parts of me to your wretchedness, and denying my unity. But at the moment of my Awakening I Know you have no power over me. The energy I gave you, I now pull back from the world, as your from is destroyed."

As you tear them, burn them or whatever, **FEEL** all the energy you poured into them streaming back into you.

Look at the object of past dependencies, and the paper chain. Say these words, and destroy them as well.

"The chain was wrought by my socially constructed mind, and left me vulnerable so that the eagles of Zeus ate my liver each day. I will break the chain. The slave-makers fashioned these dependencies to keep me asleep, fearing the god I could Become. I end these attachments."

Destroy the paper chain and the objects of dependency. As you do so imagine yourself being set free from bondage.

"I know that I am but a machine. I know that I am small in the Cosmic scale of things. I know that I am lazy and weak. But I Know that these things can be overcome. And that Knowledge lets me die to my old life, which could not contain so great a Truth."

Remove all of your clothes. Stand upon them.

Face the East.

"I Know the Secret of Shiva, that this is the age of destruction and strife, and that much can be gained very quickly to those who are True to themselves. Hail Shiva!"

Face the North.

"I Know the Secret of Saturn, that if I willingly pit myself against adversity, I will forsake the sun but gain the Stars. Hail Saturn!"

Face the West.

"I Know the Secret of Satan, that if I revolt against man's personification of the mechanistic universe, I can remake the Cosmos in the shape of my Will. Hail Satan!"

Face the South.

"I Know the Secret of Set, that if I choose the path of the god against the gods death can not take me for my form shall change. Hail Set!"

Face the main altar, and state your petition to enter the Left Hand Path.

"I call upon the Prince of Darkness in her form of Shamsan Tara, the dark goddess who causes the Self to pass beyond the grave into the next life. Guide me, oh beloved goddess, for I am dead to my past life, but have not yet Awakened to my Rebirth, where I will Love you as a goddess should be loved, and not as men think to worship the gods of their own creation."

Advance to the altar.

"The Death of my old way of life is a Shock that awakens me, and I find myself clothed in Darkness wherein all Secrets reside.

"The Prince of Darkness spoke in the far off primal time, and the Black Order Heard His Summons. I now Hear it, and Know it as a command to raise myself up by hard Work.

"I Speak, and all parts of myself for the first time in my life hear my Command and begin Working Harmoniously toward my godhood. I have placed myself on the Left Hand Path.

"I Speak, and all gods and demons, ghosts and spirits, all that have been or will ever be in this or any world, now witness my words. I have placed myself on the Left Hand Path. My courage is my protection. I Bless those who would Bless me, and aid those who would aid me, but I bow not my head to any god, man, or spirit.

"I Speak and the surface level of myself is changed by my words. I will break free of the world's distraction. I will Awaken. I will See. I will Act.

I will use the here-and-now as my single greatest Tool for Freedom! I will not forget!

"I Speak and the surface level of the world is changed by the vibration my words set up. The surface level shall slowly cease to bombard me with random waves. It will bring friction that will lead to Awareness, strife that will lead to Clarity, opportunities that will lead to Wealth, and situations that will lead to Joy. I am the Lord of this World. Slowly as I grow, each outer event will come to be a message from mySelf to myself!

"I Speak and the medial level of myself is no longer held in the grip of confusion, rather I Become the arranger awakened in old archetypes that will serve my goals, and casting out foreign bodies that enslave rather than empower. The pandemonium within shall become the kingdom of heaven. I will Become the measure of Beauty! I am the Truth!

"I Speak and the medial level of the world bows before my will. The gods and demons that man has created to rule himself, serve me. I am ABLANATHANALBA, the griffin who holds the fallen gods in his paws. Magic and propaganda spoken even a world away is now spoken to serve my greater goals!

"I Speak and with my words my Daemonic self departs into the realms of magical darkness, to speak to ancient gods and learn forbidden spells. There is not an Aethyr, a demon, a star that shall not know its presence. Into the distant past it goes, and into the future when man has spread himself across the galaxies. It will learn lore and make secret alliances in all places and times, and when it returns to me at the end of the Grand Initiation it will tell me all in the right season.

"I Speak and my voice echoes through the Daemonic world. All who have ears to Hear and will profit my Quest hasten now from tomb and temple from dreams and poems from spells and charms, that you may add to my momentum as I rise like a comet into the night. I am Choronzon your king.

"I Speak and my core self Hidden by all I have known up to now shows itself to me, and I am transformed.

"I Speak and now the Prince of Darkness looks directly upon me and I upon him, and I begin to Understand the immensity of my journey, but also the Power and Joy it shall bring. I am (State Your Name), and I acknowledge my friendship with the Prince of Darkness."

Stay still for a few moments, and then as inspiration hits you, take up the glass of sweet liquid on the altar. Hold it aloft and speak whatever your heart is filled with. As you speak, imagine your words turning into liquid and filling the cup; when the cup is full, say the words that follow. Fleck one drop of the liquid into the room for other seekers to awaken, then drain the rest of the cup.

"Here is the cup that is filled with glimpses of what might be. Here is the Dream the Prince of Darkness gave me, and as I Quest after it, all forms come into being, indeed time herself comes into being, and all is made anew. Hard is the Quest, but sweet the reward. I drink a foretaste of my future. Tasting this Sweetness, I place Trust in myself and accept the pleasures and pains of existence, as I Seek this fleeting future."

After you have drained the cup, clap your hands loudly nine times. Put away your old clothes. Sleep alone this night, and in the nude. Tomorrow put on the new clothes you have purchased, and begin the daily rites for Chaos.

CHAOS

In this section I will go over the procedure that you will perform for each section (except for the sixth, which has special rules).

First write the word CHAOS in your diary.

Beneath it you will write your nightly meditations on the topic, while sitting or standing at your altar. One night you will perform Letterism. The letter for the first week is "E."

You will say a certain phrase aloud every morning, in the following manner. You will walk to your altar, clean and ready for work. You will pick up the hand mirror, while closing your eyes. With your eyes closed you will hold the mirror in such a location that you would see your face when your eyes are opened. You will visualize a red inverse pentagram in a black field. When you have a strong picture of it, you will then open your eyes, and while looking at your face you will say your Day-Taking Phrase.

The Day-Taking Phrase for the first nine days is, "My senses are newly awakened in a vast and busy world. There is so much more going on than I ever knew, I will make this endless Chaos into a source of endless energy. I am Dattatreya, who will observe this new world, that I will become Master of all Triangles!"

You will say a certain phrase aloud every night, in the following manner. You will light your magical chamber with candles, you will cense the room with incense. You will walk to the altar and pick up the hand mirror, with your eyes closed. You will hold the mirror as before, but this time you will visualize an emerald green inverse pentagram. Open your eyes and while staring at your face, say the phrase.

The Night-Taking phrase for the first nine nights is, "Chaos has great restorative powers. It is the ground water that feeds strong trees, it is sleep that restores tired bodies. I Drink the power of Chaos each night. I am Niyohuallahuantzin, the Night Drinker." After you say the phrase write your diary entry, except on the ninth night. On the ninth night, you should perform the rite of the session, and then write your diary entry. You do not need to say the night-taking phrase on that night.

Diary entries should be your thoughts on the topic at hand. There will be a brief article on each topic, and some questions for you to consider.

Here is the essay for the Chaos session:

Chaos is of two kinds. There is simple mechanistic chaos, the mindless universe experiencing turbulence and conditions that are subject to great changes. Examples include weather patterns that are subject to great changes based on small impulses given at the right time. This type of chaos is the basis for modern Chaos theory, which the magician should acquaint him- or herself with. Books on the topic and videos on the topic should be used to feed your head this week.

The second type of chaos is human chaos. We exist most of the time in a very random state, without Will or Awareness. We happen to go to a party and meet the love of our lives, we take a drive on a whim and have a fatal auto accident, we happen to be the millionth shopper at the local mall and win a shopping spree. Despite the intention in our actions, our very lives seem to be as often made of such chaos, than as of planned and willed actions. Learning to control and accept such chaos is the challenge of the magician. It is neither something to idolize, nor to fear. Persons that cut it out of their lives can not enjoy its restorative effects, persons who never seek to control it are mere leaves in the wind.

Less than a hundred years ago, Chaos played much less of a role in human events than it does now. Sure you might meet the love of your life at a barn dance, but it would be out of a very small pool. Missing or attending a meeting in an urban environment makes for a much bigger pool of chance interactions. One of the ways the Prince of Darkness is ruling the current age is by allowing a vast amount of Chaos into the system.

Try making a list of all the Chaotic events that have really shaped your life. Did you handle them well or badly? When do you feel you need more Chaos in your life, and what do you do to get it? When you need less Chaos in your life, how do you turn it down? Make a list of all the historical events that happened so that you are who you are — how many happened because of Chaos, like the weather that knocked out the Spanish Armada, so that we mainly speak English in North America? How many of your genes were touched by a cosmic ray to give you your eye color, or whether or not you have wisdom teeth? How should you live your life knowing that the forces of Chaos may take it away tomorrow despite your plans? How do you stay awake enough so that you can snatch an opportunity that Chaos might drop in your life? What times have you taken advantage of Chaos— like finding a twenty dollar bill in the street? How many times have you (or someone you knew) stirred up Chaos in some situations just to get things going? How did it work out?

Answer as many of these questions as you can, and write about what thoughts occur to you. Write down any dreams or meaningful synchronicities.

Special magical task. If you live where this is a lottery, bet nine bucks on it, and watch the results. Write about your feelings buying the tickets, your losing (or winning), what such a windfall would mean— why Hermes is the god of the windfall in Greek mythology, and so forth.

The Ritual. The ritual should be done at night, on the ninth night. After the ritual, you should write up your feelings for the whole session, and then read the next section.

Light the candles and the incense as you do every night.

Opening. With some whistling, say the word "Eeee" nine times.

"From the roaring fire that cooled down to make the planets, I call Chaos. Oh Tiamat, oh Apep, oh Lotan. From the angry human herd I call Chaos. Oh Anger, oh Patriotism, oh Sentiment. From the infinite indeterminacy of the quantum foam I call Chaos. Oh mighty Chaos, you can not be bested, you swallow each Creation, yet you give the Freedom to Create endlessly. Oh Mighty Chaos you are the giver of happiness, because you allow the quick to pick from your cauldron the bits they desire. Oh mighty Chaos in your threefold form of Coming Into Being, Manifesting, and Passing Away— you are all that my fellow humans see, and fear. I salute Thee, Mother of us all!"

Dance and spin about the room, swirl like the forces of Chaos.

"Oh mighty Chaos, I know your secret. Men that worship you lose their souls and become animals. Men that fight you lose what they lay upon the Earth, for you Oh Entropy in your eleven-rayed might are stronger than all that stands on this Earth. But I am stronger than mankind, for I love neither Nature, which is your Holy Name Oh Chaos, nor do I love Moment, which is the Name that man huddles in against you. I live in the region of Strife, attached only to my own Becoming.

"If a Tornado comes, I will ride it as a horse, I am storm-rider! If a meteor falls, I will make weapons from its iron, I am the Opportunist; if windfall brings me trees, I gather firewood, if plague strikes my neighbor I take up his business and his family's love, if penicillin lives in my Petri dish I will make a vaccine that will save millions. I am storm-rider.

"Oh Chaos, I will learn the harsh lesson you Teach. I will rejoice in the energy you unleash. I will respect you, and I will call you seldom, but call you I will at the beginning of things, for I know that like Old Night Herself, you provide possibilities even greater than I can imagine, I who inherited imagination from Eblis Himself."

Face the altar. Now become very still and as you say each of the next nine sentences turn slowly counterclockwise, until you come to face the altar again. After each sentence blow a long deep breathe outward and imagine it raising a great wind at the corners of the Earth.

"I wreck the ships to find the loot on the beach. (Breathe). I send mild weather so that famine disappears. (Breathe) I fan the flames of the burning house. (Breathe). I blow out the forest fire. (Breathe). I blow the poor man's last dollar out of his desperate hand. (Breathe) I lift the kites of the sick children (Breathe). I blow down the bridge at rush hour. (Breathe) I lift the falling jet liner. (Breathe) I blow the scent of a long-lost memory to the dying woman, so that she Remembers herself, and passes with the possibility of Immortality. (Breathe)

"I, who am barely more than a machine, make my Pact with Chaos from which I have just emerged. Hail Lady Chaos! I accept your gift of Freedom, and give you the Gift of my actions, which since I am not a god can not help but release more Chaos than I can see. I am the Lord of Air and Darkness."

Closing. With great sibilancy whisper the word "Eeee" nine Times.

ORDER

First write the Word ORDER at the top of your diary. The letter for this session is "S."

The Day-Taking phrase is, "I am Adam, who Orders all things in the Garden of his Mind, and then drawn by Knowledge beyond dualities, ventured forth to Name and experience all of the Cosmos. I am the Master of Words, blessed is my friend Nechesh!"

The Night-Taking phrase is, "I am Lilith, equal of Adam, who Taught Adam magic and love and lust. I am the Secret that when almost all is Known, the Unknown is the greatest stimulant. I am the Mistress of Substance, wise is my brother Nechesh!"

The essay for Order follows.

The four aspects to the concept of Order are the power of Ordering, and the limitation of Ordering, the discovery of unconscious Ordering, the secret of Ordering. Let's look at each and then consider questions to stimulate your meditations.

The power of Ordering. To do any job, you need an orientation. You have to know when to do things, what the priorities are, and what the secrets of success are. As you do the job, you discover how to improve the job, and this causes you to produce a new Ordering. Sadly we don't get much of an orientation for Life. We stumble on, creating new rules. Occasionally we happen across an idea that really makes our lives better—like buy your groceries and pay your rent out of the paycheck *first*. Slowly we gain power in the world, because of our rules. Now being the good herd animals we are, we try to push our rules on others, and resent it like hell when others try to do this to us. We seldom grasp that choosing the correct ordering approach can make any job easier, and that the number one job we have as Initiates is a kind of self ordering. Only when we understand that the ordering of ourselves is the only hope we have of getting any self-imposed jobs done, does Initiation begin.

The Limitations of Ordering. To truly control a thing we need to know its name and numbers. This is not an "occult" principle. It's a day-to-day principle, like knowing how to use your ATM or how to find a friend's apartment. Now in the objective world, if our information is out of date or incorrect, we know pretty rapidly. The ATM eats our bank card, we knock at the wrong door. In the subjective world, we often don't know when the information has changed. We picture ourselves as younger than we are, and therefore don't work with urgency (after all we'll do it later), we castigate ourselves for a fault that we no longer have (like an anorexic hating herself for eating too much), or we will have adopted a silly model of the self and then made our self confirm to it. Without a real picture of who we are, we can neither use who we are to change the world, nor have a clue as to how to change ourselves. Thus we must challenge notions of who we are, all the time. This frees us from the snares of ordering.

The Discovery of Unconscious Ordering. We think that we are in charge of our actions, and that our actions follow a rational pattern. Often we are not in charge of our actions. For example a rational mind might want to sign up with a math class from the ugly old gent that has written 400 theoretical papers, but we sign up for the one taught by the pretty young TA. The Initiate is always on the lookout for sets of rules that are not his command. When he discovers these rules, he can set himself free—for example by taking the class from the ugly old gent, and getting private tutoring from the pretty young TA. Be on the lookout for hidden parts of yourself that Order things before "you" get a chance to.

The Secret of Ordering. Ordering exists as a ladder. It comes into being for a brief willed instant, and makes a great deal of energy available out of Chaos. If you make use of that instant, you can punch yourself up to another level of being. The Ordering of the world should not be the same when you are 18 as when you are 27 or 36 or 108. Non-initiates cling to one Order. Fools try to survive with none. Each new Order represents a plan to action, as you seek to impose its beauties and symmetries on the Chaos of the world. Between each person trying to make his or her own place of sense there is sometimes fighting, sometimes agreement, and in magical moments Flow of certain energies or information between the lifeworlds.

Questions for your meditation. Remember that these are only a starting point.

Make a list of all the synonyms and antonyms you can think of for "Order." What are your thoughts and feelings about each? Try to remember the times you became conscious in a strange place, and the sense of relief you had when you figured out where you were— could you remember that feeling very strongly and charge a Symbol with it? Could such a Symbol be useful for regaining coherence after death? What have you gained by putting things in Order? What kind of interpersonal conflicts have you solved by making some boundaries or rules? How did it feel to do so? Why do you think so many creation myths begin with a semidivine hero killing a personification of Chaos and making a world? Is the idea of "world" different than those myths where the world is spoken into place? What forms of Order, for example rhythm in music, make you happy? What forms can you simply not stand?

Magical tasks. To feed your head, get some good scholarly books on cognition and human development— MIT Press offers several. Rent some videos with fractals, or look at some art that shows the beauty of mathematics. Clean up your house, put your files in order, do many little mundane activities that involve sorting, ordering, and arranging.

The Ritual.

Fashion a Square of parchment. On one side write the numbers, on the other the letters that follow:

A	D	A	M		20	1	24	3
D	A	R	A		1	20	13	24
A	R	A	D		37	15	20	1
M	A	D	A		26	40	63	48

Fix the sheet to your forehead so that the letters face outward.
Opening. Hiss the word "Esss" nine times as sibilantly as possible.
Both say and Visualize the words that follow.

56

"I fall into a vast fog as burning meteor, my fire clears the fog and I find myself in a great jungle, life abounds here, strange and wonderful, I hear its cries, I smell the flowers, I rise as a burning man. My Name is my Name, it came from the first sound."

As you say this, the flames cease.

Pick up the hand mirror and look at your face. Say the following.

"My name is Adam, and I will name all things by their True Name, so that I may Know them and Command them. This is a Secret.

"My Name is Dara, and I will not be fixed by any set of names, but I will seek to Know which names for which times. This is a greater Secret.

"My name is Arad, and I will have power over who knows my name and how they use it. This is a greater Secret still.

"My name is Mada, and I will have access to Power that is beyond Names, and I will see clearly for that Power. That Power is myself, that part which even I can not Name. This is a greater Secret still.

"My true name is Unknown to me, but I shall strive ceaselessly in this world, erecting monuments of glory out of marble and human hearts, out of gardens and spoken words, out of memories and achievements to that Name, so that as I leave this world, I will look back upon them and Know the Unknown. And with that Name, I will control the next world. This is the Greatest Secret of All."

Drink a goblet full of apple juice. Leave a small amount in the bottom of the cup.

With the index and middle fingers of each hand flick a few drops in the direction indicated while speaking the words.

"To the West I send my Work. Ancient tombs open and ancient sorcerers drink the work, and I am part of their Ordering, as my ancient bones will drink in a thousand years. They Live for a moment and their ancient Spells shall be my mine to command when the time is right.

"To the South I send my work. Farmers and labors taste this sweetness, and are renewed, to serve the role that fate has given them. When I eat of their labors I shall be Restored in mind and body.

"To the East I send my work. Soldiers take courage at the Taste, and they shall bear arms in true causes, and lay down arms if they should face me.

"To the North I send my Work. Poets and story tellers are Inspired by my work, and fashion for me the songs I Need for Joy and Inspiration when the time is right."

Lay the goblet on the altar, and speak from your heart about what you are willing to give yourself. How will you put your life in Order to achieve your goals?

After you have spoken from your heart say,

"The Seal on my forehead makes me the ever-young, ever-fresh soul that may look upon wonders, and speak of them truly and without prejudice to my ancient soul. If I keep this sense of wonder I shall be ever young! If I keep this sense of honesty, I shall be powerful! If I remain this brave, I shall be very wise. As my young self is True to my old soul, so the whole of me shall be True to the Prince of Darkness, and I will be His Eyes. As my young self is True to my old soul so shall I attract companions from the vast reaches of the Earth who will be True to me and be my Eyes. Hail Beauty! Hail Order! Hail that which Creates Beauty and Order! I am the Master who does make the grass green, and who Orders the planes and angles!

"I am the Truth! I am the measure of Beauty!"

Closing. Hiss the word "Esss" nine times with great sibilancy.

Remove the seal from your forehead, put it aside. You will wish to burn it and the seal you use during the eighth session, and hide their ashes in a secret place. Write your impressions in your diary, and then read about the next nine-day session.

CLARITY

First write the word CLARITY in your diary. The letter for this session is "L."

The Day-Taking phrase is, "I am Odysseus, who travels far, who fears nothing, who is steadfast in his purpose, and blends all aspects of Life aright! I am the spiritual son of Ithax, Herald of the Titans, who stole Fire from the gods under his name of Forethought."

The Night-Taking phrase is, "I am Penelope, who is Love, who is Purpose, who is the Knower of Riddles and the teacher of Craft. I am the spiritual daughter of Pallas Athene. I make the place of refuge that can not be taken, and what I desire will come to me, even if jealous gods wish it not so."

The essay for clarity follows.

Over the last eighteen days, you will have had certain experiences that you have had all your life, sudden moments of clarity. These may have come when you sat down each night to write in your diary, they may have come while you drove to work, they may have come because you overheard a snatch of conversation. It was a great moment, wasn't it?

Such moments of understanding are called Clarity. You can See clearly. It is not an intense physical pleasure, such as orgasm, but it does have a physical component. (Such moments are rare in sickly bodies.) It is not entirely a mental pleasure, but there is a similar experience — such as the mental pleasure you have when you "find" the word you have been looking for. (Such moments seldom happen to unexercised minds.) It is not an overwhelming emotional pleasure, but it is like one— perhaps the feeling you have when you have picked out just the right gift for a loved one. (Such moments seldom come to people who have overlooked their emotional-intuitive development.) It is not entirely a triumph of the will, but feels like it— perhaps the moment your suggestion was adopted by your boss. (Such moments rarely come to those who have not had success in reshaping the objective universe.) Such moments *Unify* the body, the mind, the heart, and the will. From such moments, the possibility of Becoming a potent, powerful, independent, and immortal essence comes.

At such times, you always feel like you will never forget. This new realization will be yours for all time. Unfortunately, such is seldom the case. Just bumping into someone on the street can lose the moment for you forever.

That is because such realizations are not part of the Order of the World. They belong to the world of Mind.

Initiation consists of two activities: preparing to have such moments of Clarity, and remaking yourself so that you can keep such moments. The first is esoterically the mystery of Travel. You have to go through the world, poke your nose into a lot of things, use your smarts to get out of jams, and even be willing to suffer torments sublime like Odysseus listening to the Sirens. The second is the mystery of the Vessel. You have to reconstruct your life to keep your Revelations. This involves learning memory techniques, being sure that you put your ideas in practice, not talking about sacred things to idiots (so that you gain a sense of what some things are worth), and learning to create things (such as art) that help you Remember what you have seen as much as writing down your ideas in your diary. The Etruscan word "*Althanulus*," the holy vessels of the priest, is a guide to what you need to reshape yourself as. It is related to the pre-Greek word that became "Athene" goddess of wisdom. She always is giving wisdom to the worthy, creating crafts, and putting her ideas into practice. If you wish a less esoteric maxim, try "Change your mind and keep the change!"

People who do not restructure themselves to keep their moments of Clarity become addicted to certain experiences. They buy tons of occult books for the "rush" they get reading each chapter, but at the end of the book they know nothing. They spend significant money on occult seminars, have a great time— and the day the weekend is over, their understanding is as well. They go through friends at a fast pace, excited by the brief flashes that each new friend must bring, but unwilling to work at the long work of friendship, which produces slower much deeper flashes of Clarity.

Such addicts are useful to us, because they call the occult world into being with their seeking. But we must profit from their example, rather than join their starry-eyed horde. All of the readers of this book have some of that tendency in them, many will be ruled by it (and toss this book after its first reading. To those who are buying this volume in a used book store, Uncle Setnakt sends his belated greetings. You might send a note to Rûna-Raven and ask about their new titles.)

For most, the most useful moments of Clarity come in the mode of being they find most difficult. If they are very intellectual/logical, Clarity will come in emotional/intuitive activities. If they are very spontaneous, clarity will come in highly structured moments. This principle of **polarization** is one of the most useful and difficult of all things to be learned on the Left Hand Path.

It is useful at this time to consider the idea of Synchronicity.

We have all had the experience of the meaningful coincidence. We are thinking of an old friend, and suddenly she calls us. We are mentioning a favorite song only to suddenly turn on the radio to hear it. Two friends send us postcards on the same day. Something feels "magical" in such an occurrence, yet it would be hard to say what.

What does occur when we experience synchronicity?

There are two separate occurrences that feed each other, and if we so Will it, feed our coming into being. The first is the sense of wonder. This feeling is very precious to the modern magician. We live for the most part in a world without wonder. We may say we are magicians, that we "believe" in magic, but in reality that is not the case. We live for the most part in the dense reality of our neighbors. Only at certain moments do we glimpse reality being loosened. We need to breath in such moments to undo the damage to our subjective universe that the sleeping world does on a daily basis.

The second occurrence is a Sensing of the Magical Link. When we can feel that spontaneous movement from subjective to objective universe — such as in the example of thinking of an old friend just before her phone call — there is a moment of *stretching* from the Subjective pole to the Objective one. This is the feeling, the taste, of magic. You should learn what this feels like, you should strive to make it a body memory. Then it is easier to access when you want to "Do" magic again. Perhaps you may wish to come up with a word or gesture that enables you to catch this body memory.

Now if synchronicity is a good thing, what do we need to do in order to experience more of it? Well a couple of things. Number one is to attack the density of reality around you. If you live in a world that is completely bound by the same patterns, things will tend to seize up around you. Do you always eat, sleep, go to work at the same time? Do you go to the movies on the same night, call your friends on the same night, have one night to answer your magical correspondence? Break from these patterns. Remember to rebel from your routines. If your life is too tight, there is no room for magic to manifest.

A second way to increase synchronicity is to study it. Better still, study it with a friend. Get a book on the topic, both of you read it at the same time (already creating a synchronicity). Talk about meaningful coincidences in the past that have shaped your lives. Watch for the meaningful coincidences in your lives now. The few weeks you spend on the project will up the number and type of synchronicities in your life. This will level off after awhile, but the ability to get secret communication from the unknown will be yours for a long time.

It would be easy to define the source of synchronicities with the Unconscious, since we don't have a particularly good definition of that. But a more useful source for the Left Hand Path is the impelling sense of magical curiosity called Rûna which is Understood to be an active force in the world of those who Seek Becoming by a Quest for the Unknown. Synchronicities that are very profound should be noted in your magical diary. This helps you begin to be connected to a world more aligned with your own Becoming than with the world of dense nonmagical reality.

If you wish to know more about Rûna, the V° Word of Stephen Edred Flowers, you should read his book *Rûnarmâl I*. (See the Resources section).

Here are the questions for your meditations. Remember these are only starting points.

When in your life did you feel you really had it all 'figured out'? What did you do with that realization? What is the most important thing you have ever discovered about the world on your own? How did you remember it? What is an important thing you thought you would never forget, then you forgot, then you remembered later? Why do the Greek goddesses that inspire art have the name of 'Reminders' (=Muses)? Are there certain physical locations where you have had more breakthroughs than elsewhere? What do these places have in common? Have you had a friend or loved one have the same breakthrough at the same as you, although far away? Why can't you do that on a regular basis? Are you addicted to the "rush" of Understanding, but have no way of keeping it? Why does Clarity that stays with us come from the most unexpected places?

Magical Tasks. Read about synchronicity (if you can, use the book in the resource section). Get your friends, relatives, co-workers to talk about their moments of "enlightenment"— or about moments of synchronicity in their lives. Get as much discussion as you can about this around you. Buy yourself a small globe to use during the Rite. Buy yourself a piece of art that represents to you what you feel you want to become. If you can, have it gift wrapped, and open it just before you begin the Rite.

The Ritual

Opening. Say the words "Lalll, Leellll, Lilll, Lolll, Lulll, Lolll, Lilll, Leellll, Lalll." Say it loudly and slowly, vibrating the "L" sound.

Hold your arms up in such a manner as to suggest that you are a goblet.

"I will become the *Althanulus*, with the help of my Daughters— Zelos, Kratos, Bia, and Nike, I am Become the perfect cup awaiting the elixir my divine self has brewed since before the beginning of time."

Picture a giant hand pouring a liquid into the Cup of yourSelf. Then put your arms down.

Light a black candle.

"This flame is the Light of Clarity that I have often Lit in my Life. It is the only Light I trust, because it comes from within. It burns through my Life, my Lust, my Love. I am the Flame and the Keeper of the Flame. This is the Model of existence that the Prince of Darkness bequeathed to my race.

"The Dark-Light grows. It burns in my Thoughts, it burns in my Words, it burns in my Deeds.

"At three angles I Light this, and I am a new Force come into being, full of action. At six points I exalt it, and achieve all by not-doing. At nine points, I carry it back to another realm and affect all worlds."

Warm your left hand over the candle.

"I am Lightning the perfect Thought. I am Thunder the perfect Mind."

Imagine a great storm cloud rising out of your body. It floats up over your dwelling, and you float with it. Draw your hand back from the fire.

Imagine the storm cloud growing bigger, until it covers the Earth. Black lightning crackles around the cloud, then as you speak, it will strike the Earth. Pick up the small globe and speak the words.

"Lightning flashes, and it awakens those who will test me and make me strong. They begin moving toward me, enlivened by the lightning.

"Lightning flashes, and it awakens those who will enrich me, and they move toward me bearing tribute.

"Lightning flashes, and it strikes me, and awakens me to my potential!

"Lightning flashes, and it burns my enemies to a crisp.

"Lightning flashes, and ancient gods descend the spiral stair to Teach me.

"Lightning flashes, and it strikes me, and welds the parts of myself together against the power of Time!

"Lightning flashes, and it frightens away fools and parasites and time wasters.

"Lightning flashes, and shows what is Hidden in the Night.

"Lightning flashes, it strikes me and carries me off to another realm where I will Work at lightning speed!"

Put the globe down.

"The storm has passed, but other storms will come. I will learn in storm and I will learn in calmness. I am he who makes the lightning flash and the thunder speak her name. But amidst the storm of this world, I am calm. For I know what I must be."

Look at the art you bought yourself. Be quiet and still. If after awhile, you feel you have more to say, speak from the Heart. When you have spoken, say the Closing.

Closing. Say the words "Lalll, Leellll, Lilll, Lolll, Lulll, Lolll, Lilll, Leellll, Lalll." Say it quietly and quickly with great crispness of speech. Write your impressions in your diary, and then read about the next nine-day session.

LIFE

First write the word LIFE in your diary. The letter for this session is (once again) "E."

The Day-Taking phrase is, "I am Kali the devourer, my past is my food, the world's past is my food. Everyone I see today will die in Time, every building I walk through will crumble, every human institution will fade. I am Shakti, I am Tara, I am Sodasi. The world is my Play!"

The Night-Taking phrase is, "I am Tezcatlipoca, my footprint is the Seven Stars, I am Huemac, ancient god of Tula whose daemonic self is overpoweringly Strong, I am Moquequeloa, the Mocker, who created men for his endless amusement, I am Cetl who controls all that is dark, dangerous, and cold. The future reflects me!"

The essay for Life follows.

Many people waste their lives waiting for a moment that never comes. They labor very hard, socking away their money for a perfect retirement, and then when they build that cabin by the lake discover they have inoperable cancer.

Others never give their lives a second thought. They spend all their money when they get it, use every opportunity for enjoyment, and face old age broke, and worse still having accomplished nothing in their lives.

The Initiate knows that adult life falls into three parts. There's a time of struggle to establish yourself, a time when great action against the status quo of the world is possible, and a time of reflection and preparation for death. Knowing that the key to doing this well is having the right amount and type of challenges in his or her life, the Initiate sets up to have each phase of his or her life contain the right sorts of semidivine effort (see below). He or she will have gathered the resources necessary for the long fight, including virtues and magical power.

The Initiate does this by making the right effort and making sure that he or she gets the rewards of these efforts.

One of the simplest ideas that mature human beings have is that Reward should be tied to Effort. Human beings that don't understand this spend their lives over their parents' garage. Most of the real frustration that permeates our world comes from the separating of reward and effort. An Understanding of the Doctrine of Effort is an Understanding of commitment to action in the Objective Universe, which is a core principle of the Left Hand Path. I will point out the types of effort, the effect that Sorcery has on effort, and finally the application of the doctrine to society and employment.

Types of effort. There are four types of effort: animal, human, heroic, and semidivine. Each is characterized by the source of guidance, the limits of freedom, the voluntarism required, and the type of reward obtained. <u>Animal effort</u> is the effort required of humans to perform thoughtless tasks under close supervision. The mantra associated with animal effort is "Would you like fries with that?" The job is totally defined, creativity is discouraged, if performance isn't up to a low objective standard people are dismissed, and there are no rewards for excelling in your performance. The job would be done by a trained monkey, except that trained monkeys are too expensive. <u>Human effort</u> is the effort that most people hope to achieve, and almost half the population does so. It is the sphere of effort in a closely supervised environment, where excellence pays off. Here are the jobs where, if you work hard, you will be rewarded by greater opportunities of freedom (*i.e.*, your superiors leave you alone), there is some recognition for your creativity, and increased monetary benefits. Within broad well-defined parameters, you are rewarded for voluntarism. <u>Heroic effort</u> is the effort required when you place yourself in a difficult situation for the self-transformation obtained. This is the type of effort that begins to set man's rulers apart from the herd. It requires freedom of action, followed by submission. A perfect example would be someone volunteering to join the Marines. Voluntarism ends after that. The drill sergeant doesn't ask you to volunteer to get up at 4:30 in the morning. The rewards for heroic effort are the acquisition of human virtues like Bravery, Determination, Patience, and so forth. <u>Semidivine effort</u> is, of course, the most difficult. It requires constant voluntarism. You put yourself in a difficult situation to transform yourself, that is not supervised but *suggested*. This is in an environment where an Ideal is held before you, but the achievement of the Ideal is up to your own actions.

Effects of Sorcery. Now as magicians we are lazy and greedy, so we want to get reward without effort. If we are any good at all at this, we usually give up effort altogether. However, if we decide to put our Sorcery in the service of our selves, we can accomplish a miracle in the above schema. Sorcery has the power to *transmute* the arena to the next higher notch. We may be working at a burger place, but with magic we can cause human opportunities to open up. (This doesn't mean we are smart enough/tough enough to take such opportunities.) We may have a simple human job, but with magic we can manifest a heroic job (for example, we go from being a desk jockey to having a globe-traveling job that requires much, and that rewards with both money and self transformation). We can even change a heroic job, like being a PSYOP in Vietnam, to a semidivine job, like starting an Aeon. Properly Understood and applied, Sorcery can change the playing field. This is the "break" that Black Arts give us.

But the opposite is sadly true as well. We can use our magical powers simply to make our lives easier, and then fill that ease with more time to pursue the mind-numbing amusements of our neighbors. We can change a heroic job into a human career. We can turn a human career into an animal job. The possibility for de-evolution is always around us. Our fellow humans are too stupid and weak to know this, or they would have dragged the world down a long time ago. But we, the Elect, Know. We can make things too easy on ourselves, so that we merely sleep.

Application of the Idea of Effort. As an Initiate precedes down the Left Hand Path, he or she develops the Need to remake the objective universe more and more in the image of his or her values. This means that we have to modify what we do for a living, since that is where we spend the most of our time. The first modification that we have to bring about, is to be sure that the environment provides Reward for Effort. One can not pursue an LHP life in a system that either ignores or penalizes effort. The second task is more subtle. We must modify the environment so that it allows us to gain personal reward for our efforts. For example it isn't that hard to get raises for jobs well done (millions of non-magicians manage this), but it is hard to get companies to provide places for our Selfish development. Learning to train your company to think it's a good idea to help you get your law degree, or your engineer's certification, and so forth is the Great Work. Your efforts, which will be hard, benefit yourself, and you will have changed your employer into your tool.

We also realize that any force outside ourselves that draws rewards from our efforts is a Right Hand Path force. The primary examples are governments, who take our money for their ends. The game that these forces play is to make us debate which of their ends is the better one— do we spend this money on government might (military) or government co-dependence (social programs)? As long as we debate this, they draw in the shekels. The Left Hand Path Initiate must oppose (in well thought-out legal means) these forces on the one hand. This is much, much tougher than the easy antinomianism of making fun of the church. But a second more subtle task exists: we must Do the action that the government has hooked us with.

If we are really concerned about social injustice, we have to act in the trenches, by feeding the poor. If it's an environmental issue that pulls our strings, we must be in the front line. It is not enough to oppose injustice, we must Work to produce justice. The lessons learned in changing the world are the lessons that will work in changing ourSelves.

Questions for your meditations: Remember these are starting points only.

What would be the ideal lifestyle to pursue Initiation? What things do you want to own in the world? Do you have the right kind of money, funds, and insurance? If the Prince of Darkness appeared before you tonight and offered you everything you wanted, would you take Him up on it? What if he had made the same offer to you nine years ago— what kind of life would you have chosen? What do your changing desires tell you about yourself? Why do you feel the need to justify what you want to another? Why is that social chain much stronger than religious and political disapproval? Why is it important to stand up for the rights of groups you don't like? How would you want your friends to remember you? How much can you change your field of endeavor? How would you like to see the experience that you are undergoing be brought to the field you work in? How would you have your enemies remember you?

Magical tasks. You have two magical jobs during this session. The first is to buy a cheap, wind-up clock that ticks very loudly. Do this the first day, or before. Put it on the altar, so that its ticking annoys you while you write in your diary. Listen to its ticking as much as you can during the session. The second task is a visualization. As you drift off to sleep, imagine yourself falling into your body, and the bed beneath. Picture your whole town being sucked in after you. Then each day, look around town for images and ideas you may have seen during your dreams. Note these in your diary. During this week read about annuities, IRAs, 410-K, investing in real estate, and so forth.

The Ritual

Cover all the clocks and time-keeping devices you can see in your magical chamber, except for the clock you bought. Place a small pastry and four birthday candles on your altar.

Opening. Say the word "Ex" nine times very precisely like the ticking of the clock.

"I have looked upon the Need for urgency. Everyone I have spoken to this week will die, I will die, there is so much to be done. In the Name of Anubis I have obtained this night the fourfold ring that Fafnir guards. Its fourfold shape gives me increase and smites my enemies. It is the link by which the Black Order doth rule the world. Anubis whispered to me, 'The access to the Divine is through Time.'

"I must bind time to my Will, otherwise it will bind me to my Death."
Smash the clock with a hammer.

"From timelessness I came, to timelessness I return, by the Secret of timelessness I rule over myself. The time within is slow and fast, it changes at my Will and can even flow backward. The time without is a serpent swallowing its own tail. That serpent I have drawn around the

65

letters in my meditations. If I can but ride the Serpent, I can know the Absolute."

Unwrap the pastry and put it on the altar. Stick the four birthday candles into the cake, and as you light each one speak the words that follow.

"In the surface level of time, I appear cool and powerful because of my great sense of Purpose. This image soothes others around me. I can take the time to smell the roses, yet I always return to my Task.

"In the medial level of time, I seethe with urgency. My thoughts and feelings urge me to do more, be more, go further. In my thoughts and feelings I accept the inevitability of my own death as an adviser.

"In my core self, I Know that simultaneity and eternity are the sides of one coin, the Pantacle with which I enchant the universe.

"My daemonic self draws near, and tells me its plan. Tonight it will travel back in time to represent me in all the magical workings that have shaped the world. My magic is at the Roots of all things."

After having lit all the candles, say the following,

"Tonight I am four angles old. Chaos and Order and Space and Time are the points of a great Door that I now step through into Eternity. The COST has been great, and greater costs follow, but none compares to the adventure ahead."

Close your eyes, make a Wish, blow out the candles.

Pull the candles from the cake. (Discard them later far from your home, and in secret.) After removing the candles say the following,

"The only Indulgence for my hard path to Becoming a god, is that I will allow myself to completely forgive myself and love myself. I eat my past, and it nourishes me. I Remember things long forgotten."

Eat the small pastry.

"Fortified by this feast, I am prepared for the hard work in this fourth great age. Everyday I feed myself memories, and every day I am Stronger for what lies ahead."

Closing. Say the word "Ex" nine times in a drawn-out manner.

Clean up the area, write your impressions in your diary, and read about the next nine nights.

CREATION

First write the word CREATION in your diary. The letter for this session is "O."

The Day-Taking phrase is, "I am Baal-Saphon, who cut the twenty-two letters in rock for Dido's race. All mysteries of writing are mine, and I create new worlds as others write. I dwell upon Mountain Saphon at the Pole, and release hurricanes against the ships that do not honor my Name."

The Night-Taking phrase is, "I am Dositheos, who like Prometheus brought a Gift from a Secret place. I gave my gift to my fellow men before I departed to the Secret Region. I gave them a ladder to the Holy Headless One, that they may speak as he, that they make worlds and Aeons. Invoke often, I told them. AOTH ABRAOTH BASYM ISAK SABAOTH IAO."

The essay for Creation follows.

Firstly I will look at the idea of Creation in a Left Hand Path context, and then I will look at the emotional and ideational adjustments that a Self-Created god will need to make.

The Idea of Creation. In most Right Hand Path religions the idea of Creation is the basis for the notions of Unity with the Cosmos, and the ultimate ineffectiveness of the individual. This notion is so strongly a part of our culture that it remains with people long after they have "broken" with mainstream RHP systems such as Christianity. If you doubt the power of this, try saying "We are all, after all, made of starstuff," and watch how your audience sighs. The notion of Creation has been enshrined in "scientific" thinking as well, and still rules the world.

In the Right Hand Path, Creation is best understood as the idea of *dependent origination.* This idea (held in Buddhism, Christianity, B. F. Skinnerism, Marxism— you name it) is that all things are following a course or law that existed long before the phenomena we perceive and will exist long afterward. There is no free will, and things are either here for a Purpose, or the universe is mechanistic. Either condition comes from the Right Hand Path view of Creation

Let's examine the Right Hand Path idea of *dependent origination.* (I am freely borrowing this example from Vietnamese Zen Master Tich Naht Hanh.) *Uncle Setnakt's Essential Guide to the Left Hand Path* is in your hand, because Rûna-Raven bought it, because someone made the ink and the paper, because someone cut down the tree to make the paper, because someone made the lunch of the logger who cut down the tree to make the paper, because someone gave birth to someone who made the lunch, because someone set up the political situation that caused the birth-giver's family to be wherever it was, and so forth. Or you could say that I wrote the book because I joined the Temple of Set, that Michael Aquino started because he didn't like where the Church of Satan was going, which La Vey started because a publicity man named Webber suggested that he do so, and that Webber wouldn't have done that if he hadn't have lived in San Francisco, which wouldn't be there except for its natural harbor, which wouldn't have mattered except that mankind developed sailing in the Stone Age, which they wouldn't have done except that water covers so much of the planet, which wouldn't have been the case except that Sol is a Class M Yellow Star, which wouldn't be possible if it weren't for Planck's Constant. In short nothing exists on its own, and the laws that make it not only possible but inevitable come into being the moment that universe did. Even your thoughts which arise from biological processes are connected with every bit of the progress of organic life on this planet.

The "oneness" with all, and the impermanence of the observable present, are the key Cosmological ideas of the Right Hand Path.

We would argue that they are correct for the world of Nature. The physical world does run its mechanistic course. Some would say that this is due to God, the Great Architect. Others would see it as an organic whole, such as Gaia. Others would see it as a mechanical whole. Each of these views, Christian, Wiccan, or Atheist is a Right Hand Path view that suborns the present into a consequence of the moment of Creation.

The Left Hand Path would argue that there are Principles that exist outside of the time-space law domain that permit freedom beyond the mechanistic. Such freedom inevitably leads to conflict with any set of Principles extracted from the mechanistic world, such as laws of behavior. Any sense of this Principle would therefore be seen as "Dark" or "Forbidden." This is an animal reaction to the force that allows for non-animal behavior.

If one is to survive the strongest force of the space-time continuum, which is Time, one must Create one's self. That is, one must act in ways not predetermined by one's biology, culture, and age. One's choices must lead them to states of being and types of activity that are not the slot that the world machine would create for them.

One must rebel.

It must be a *creative rebellion*. Simply doing the opposite of whatever the world machine tells you to do is not enough. It can help you realize how arbitrary the "rules" of the world are— wear your hair long when others wear it short, wear light pastels to a Goth club and Goth clothes to a golf club, wear a swastika to a synagogue's garage sale, and a Star of David to an Aryan Nation meeting— and you learn how the monkeys around you are well trained. (Don't do any of these things unless you can run like hell.)

Only in Self-Creation does the Left Hand Path exist, and only from the data learned by hard experience, once you have made the commitment to live by your choices, can you proceed down that path. The Left Hand Path begins with the realization, "I have come into being!"

Emotional and Ideational Adjustments for Creators. Simply leading a good life is not enough. There are tasks that you will want to Do, as you come to understand yourself more clearly, that would take many lifetimes to Do.

Simply thinking good thoughts is not enough. Initiation is the process of thinking the right thoughts at the right time— but happens when there is more than one thought to be thought at a given time. What happens when your own Initiation has become so dynamic that it must be thought of in terms of world-building? When you Need more than one head to think your thoughts?

World-building is not an easy skill to learn. Men are not gods, and our actions are bound by many forces that gods would not have to put up with. But in another sense, world-building is going on all the time, with everything that we do. If we decide to read a certain newspaper, we take that view into our world. If we decide to hang out with certain people and avoid the phone calls of others, we are populating our world. Our strengths and failures rest heavily on the worlds we build.

For example, if we have filled our world with good people, our ideas march forward even if we are sick in bed with the flu. If we have put our worlds together carefully, with good strong ideas, we will attract good people. If our worlds are big, we will not know boredom.

Human beings are organized around a chief flaw. There is always a secret about ourselves that we will go to any length to protect. If that

Secret is threatened, we will engage in all sort of bad behavior, which we will then justify with strong appeals to principle afterward.

Creators have to overcome this flaw, by finding an artificial principle to build a world around.

An average human's world is built around a flaw, that they maintain with "self-pity."

A magician's world is based around a Word that instructs them as fully as the emotion of self-pity does. This use of a magically-created and - chosen principle is the Secret to world building.

The principle has already been at work in you. It lies hidden in your experience, and all the good things in your life so far have adhered to that principle. It is the magnet that has given you a nucleus of friends, family, resources— all of which you may draw on to build your world.

Now as you build this world, you must not make your friends, family, and resources the front soldiers in your fight against the chaotic forces that oppose it. For the most part you must harden your mind, develop your will and courage so that you are mainly their protector.

Consider the Magus Gurdjieff. When his world was threatened by the Bolshevik revolution, which was almost its exact opposite magically speaking, he didn't run. He moved his followers to a place of safety. When World War II broke out, he didn't flee to America. He stayed with his followers and kept them safe. How strong was the world he built?

You can't go into any occult store in the world without seeing his writings or those of his students. Gurdjieff groups of all kinds thrive around the world. Even Uncle Setnakt, normally a rather egotistic fellow, bows at the great worth of Gurdjieff's Teaching.

Gurdjieff had the four things needed to make a world. First an idea, that "Truth is not forgetting!". This gave him a touchstone on what methods to pick up, which people to lure to his side, what work he had to do in his life. Second he developed a method that was hard, and — as such things must be — harder on himself than on others. Third he gave himself in true love and devotion to the people who used the harsh method on themselves. Fourth he gave up pity. Now this did not mean that his personal problems vanished overnight. It meant that he had simply Created a new assemblage from which to act, instead of where things came "naturally." Thus his love created real miracles, as opposed to the soul-sucking force called "love" in this world.

We can profit from his example. We can target "pity" as the great enemy. We can take a concept that Resonates with the idea of the Left Hand Path and make that our center point. We can be hard on ourselves, which will Teach us that it is a good thing to be hard on others. Then we will get the souls we need for the world.

If we discover that we can't do the world creation task, we can look for others that are Doing it, and help them out by taking the steps just mentioned.

This is a good time to meditate on my V° Word of Xeper. I am a Magus of the Word Xeper (pronounced "Khefer"), an English-language coinage expressing an Egyptian verb written as a stylized scarab and meaning "I

Have Come Into Being." This Word generates the Aeon of Set, and is the current form of the Eternal Word of the Prince of Darkness. To Know this Word is to know that the ultimate responsibility for the evolution of your psyche is in your hands. It is the Word of freedom, ecstasy, fearful responsibility, and the root of all Magic.

Xeper is the Word of Worlds, it describes the process of how all worlds Come Into Being. It is a Word that Creates a matrix into which it can be reUttered, both on the personal and historical levels. Each reUtterance both destroys and re-Creates the matrix into which it is Uttered or Known. It is the word of cyclic dynamism, reflecting the cycle of Manifestation → Being → Dismanifestation → Remanifestation. It effects those who Know it as a pleasurable and clear perception of their Reality, Power, and Will in both the Objective and Subjective Universes. Each moment of Knowing Xeper, that is to say of being in the place in your life where you can say, "I Have Come Into Being!" is a moment that Ouspensky describes as Objective Consciousness. It is from the moments of perceiving and acting upon Xeper, that the Left Hand Path Initiate begins the process of becoming an immortal, independent, powerful, and potent Essence, which effects the universes in many ways both causally and a-causally.

An Aeon is a world. As human beings we are familiar with many "worlds." We can talk about the "world of Thomas Jefferson" or the "world of Newton." Magical worlds are created by Words — by the verbal power of mankind to express a divine principle — which through the effect of that Utterance on the objective universe brings about the creation of the world. The Word serves as a gateway for the mind seeking to enter the world it defines, and the effect of an Utterance of a Word will cause many worlds to be reconfigured in order to Hear it. The Aeon of Set is Created by the Word "Xeper." Xeper is an Egyptian verb meaning "I Have Come Into Being." Xeper is the experience of an individual psyche becoming aware of its own existence and deciding to expand and evolve that existence through its own actions. Xeper has been experienced by anyone who has decided to seek after his or her own development.

Awareness of Xeper usually begins with a moment of rebellion against the spiritual status quo. In this sense Xeper is a "Satanic" word, and the condition that led to its re-emergence on this Earth began in the Working called the Church of Satan. Its properties transcend and are in some ways opposed to that matrix. It is the nature of Self-Creation that it continually Re-creates its matrix in the objective universe so that the subjective universe can evolve and expand. To experience that moment of Xeper, of emergent self-divinity, one must Love two things with all of one's heart. The first of these is Freedom, because only in Freedom can one take the steps (if initially only mentally) that create and limit the Self. The second thing one must Love is Knowledge. This isn't the same thing as information; this a transformative Understanding of those things within us and beyond us that determine who we are.

The symbols of Xeper are the scarab beetle and the dawning sun. The beetle is symbolic of self trust and hard work. The beetle goes through very different stages from egg to larva to pupa to beetle. Each stage has its own Work, a particular way of gathering energy and materials, particular ways of transforming them. It senses its own evolution and works toward it — even though the momentum of that evolution will change its shape radically — taking it at the appropriate time into unknown worlds and new modes of Being. The dawn is symbolic of the way the world is perceived. Unlike the followers of conventional religion who possess guidebooks that explain the world away, the Seeker after Xeper is looking for an intensification of his or her own Being so that the world may be made intelligible in his or her own light. In this darkling universe there are no lights save for those you create through your hard work, your spiritual rebellion, your seeking after the mysteries of your own choosing. When that light dawns, it will by its very nature not only give you moments of clarity about the things in your life closest to you, it will likewise show you new horizons— horizons for you and you alone to explore. This Secret was known symbolically to the Egyptians— they identified their god Xepera, the Self-Created One, with Hrumachis, the god of the Horizon. This Secret was also known (at a divine level) by Aleister Crowley, who predicted that the Aeon of Hrumachis would surpass his own.

Set, the Egyptian god of Darkness, is the Divine origin of the Word. Set's name ultimately means the "Separator" or "Isolator." His chief enemies are the gods of Stasis and Mindlessness. The first of these is Osiris, Death himself. Set's slaying of Osiris has a twofold significance for the seeker of Xeper. Firstly this represents the slaying of old thought patterns, the dethroning of those internal gods that we have received from society. On a second level this was the act by which Set, alone of all the gods of ancient Egypt, became deathless. The Left Hand Path is a quest to Become an immortal, independent, potent, and powerful Essence.

Set's other enemy is the demon of mindless chaos, Apep. Set is said to slay this creature every night just before dawn. This symbolizes overcoming self doubt and delusion, of acting at the times of greatest despair, and not succumbing to the self-hypnotizing engines of mankind. Set achieves (on a divine level) this isolation from the universe so that he may say, "Xeper" = "I Have Come Into Being." Each of these breaks — the break from the dead past (by slaying Osiris) and the break from the confused present (by slaying Apep) — is done for the sake of a self-determined future. One of Set's cult titles, Set-Heh, means God of Unending Futurity.

Set did not receive the aid of other gods in his two quests, nor does Set give aid to those who seek to emulate these quests on a human level. Those who struggle (like Set) with the principle of Xeper are of his Essence. Their actions are essentially the same. Those who want to share their quests and pool their knowledge seek after Set's chief tool of His Aeon, the Temple of Set. It is the most concentrated environment for the study of Xeper, both as noun and verb. As such those who are effected by the power of their own Xeper will seek to enhance and protect the Temple.

Xeper can not be studied as an abstract intellectual idea, it must be experienced. One can read about Justice, or one can hope for it, but to truly Know Justice you must bring it into Being. One can read about Xeper, as your interest in secret things has brought you to do. You can hope for it. Or you can seek the solitary self-transformation that will cause you to experience it. The Temple of Set represents a concentration of the Aeon; like Set himself, it does not answer prayers, and by its very Being provides challenges for those who would seek after the Word of Xeper. It is the embodiment of the Emerald Dawn enVisioned by a German LHP order, the Fraternitas Saturni. We are not necessarily a "Satanic" order, other than we Understand that for Initiation on the Left Hand Path to be effective for those who have just begun Work on that path, the antinomian aspect of the Work does Need to be fulfilled by some means. The imagery of the Black Arts provides that Need for many, but it likewise can be limiting as it is mastered. Our predecessor was caught by this trap, and we hope — by exploring the manifestations of the principle of Xeper in many cultures and times and in our own creations — to have much further horizons. Diabolical imagery is useful only in a culturally-bound antinomian sense; beyond this it represents a new stasis to be discarded.

Xeper. Now, an Egyptian verb, like an English verb, can have several forms depending on its number, tense, voice, and mood. You can have a verb such as *run* which can be conjugated (I run; you run; he, she, or it runs; we run — I am running — I ran — etc.). There are about 140 forms for an English verb (I remember this because my Junior High School Latin teacher often made us write the full conjugation of English verbs when he was mad at us). We happen to know the tense and person of the verb Xeper from the sentence Xepera Xeper Xeperu. It is first person, stative. Now while you're trying to remember your High School grammar as to what tense "stative" is— you won't. We don't have the tense in English. It refers to a past event that modifies a current state. We do have first person, of course; that means that "I" did it.

The proper translation of the verb Xeper is "I Have Come Into Being." Now there are some implications of this that we in the Temple have not yet considered. Firstly the verb refers to a moment that *HAS* happened that explains why we are here. When you write or speak or think the word "Xeper" you are talking about something that has taken place. You are not talking about something taking place at the moment of the speech act. Xeper is **NOT** a continuous process. It is a series of events, whose presence we sense either through reason, or through divine apprehensions. We are aware that **something** has occurred to give us the particular Being we have at any moment. We are aware that whatever the great shaping potential of that **something**, we don't have that potential at this moment. In short we are aware that we have had a moment wherein we acted as gods. We did something divine — we had some peak experience — we made some life-altering choice— and it has produced the creatures we are now. Now this produces two great realizations. First, we are aware that we have a capacity beyond wherever and whenever we are right now to both Limit and Create ourselves. All moments of Xeper both Limit and Create ourselves— or to use both of those ideas at the same time, all moments of Xeper Isolate ourselves from the Cosmos. Second, we want to

72

do this again. Humankind wants the Divine. In erroneous religions this desire is a return to the Divine in one way or another (either by union or by being in the divine presence in some place with far too much harp music). Well that doesn't work— you can't go back to the state where Xeper last occurred. You can't go back to a previous divine state any more than you can fold an oak back into an acorn. You can only go forward to another divine state. If you want to both achieve and experience your godhood, you've got to go forward. In our Earthly incarnation we never fully experience the divine moment; only through magical introspection do we discover that we have passed through them, and can therefore say (with both happiness and terror) "I Have Come Into Being." In the Bremmer-Rhind papyrus this idea is reflected in the fact that Xepera's first two children are Shu (Reason) and Tefnut (Peak Emotions). Through these two **Human** experiences we can detect the divine, and having detected it learn to Work with it to have more divine experiences.

Now the first question is: How do I have more divine experiences? Xeper happens to every sapient being. Most humans (and most of us most of the time) stumble across those experiences that would set up the conditions so that they could later say, "Xeper" if they had a large enough brain to hold the concept. The experience might be going into a drugstore to buy a malted milk and meeting the person who becomes your spouse for the next fifty years. Well, that was a divine moment, it both Limited and Created your Life. A Christian would say it was the hand of God, a Hindu would invoke Karma. But we know who did it— that man or woman we face in the mirror everyday. The scary thing for all humans — and in fact the reason they/we invented religion in the first place — is that **most** divine experiences occur blindly. So most humans either ask some fairy tale on bended knee not to give them bad experiences, or if they're a little braver try to influence them with magic, or try to deny them by exerting the meaningless nature of the Cosmos. But the Left Hand Path initiate, knowing that only through such experiences can he or she find the metamorphosis that our philosophy finds both achievable and desirable, seeks out the divine experience. I can't tell you where to find yours. If you did what I did, you would mainly find that it didn't work. That is because of the individualistic nature of Xeper (remember?— First Person verb).

This tells you many things about Xeper, the verb. It is **NOT** continuous. All events do not feed it equally. It is not fully under conscious control, rather consciousness and emotion arise from it; but these can and must be used to seek more of it. This means that Xeper is **NOT** simple self-development or self-improvement, but that those things chosen rationally can put us in the place where Xeper can occur. All sapient beings experience Xeper, but those who can name it and Understand its purpose have a much better chance of achieving it. The paths to it are absolutely personal, but some of its properties (such as being fed/triggered by peak experiences) lead to certain group functions as facilitators. It Limits you— Divine decisions always involve a road not taken. It Creates you— Divine decisions always lead to much more than can be rationally deduced. When you can say "Xeper" you are in some way a different person.

The noun "Xeper" — that thing we speak of as our "Xeper" — is likewise an Egyptian noun. It is usually translated into English as *manifestation*, or "The thing that happened." The plural of the noun is Xeperu. When we talk about our "Xeper" we are talking about a very large thing indeed— and we usually (in our normal sluglike mode) give very little thought to it. Yet if we simply Become aware of Xeper— our personal magical and philosophical horizons greatly expand. Many magicians in the Temple of Set take justifiable pride in the magical items they create. It's easy to see one's magic in a necklace one makes. However as magicians what we do is make a very large magical object, existing on many levels of reality. Our entire lives considered at any moment is a Xeper, a manifestation. If you can think of all the things that you've wrought — changes in your mind/body complex, your recognition, your reputation — all of those things that represent what you have brought to this Earth — as a giant talisman, then you've got a handle on Xeper, the noun. Many of you may have written a Rune to pull something — gold or love — out of the Unmanifest. That Rune is a tiny, tiny version of the great talisman your Xeper is. The creation of Xeper is the Working whereby we attract what we're going to get in this life, and the divine memory we will have of this life.

Xeper, the noun, is **the extension of existence to a further level of Being**. These extensions can be a thought that you've pulled to a developed conscious level from an intuition— which would represent two levels of being in your Subjective Universe. These extensions can be what others think of you. The extensions are particularly evident in actions that represent a first or personal best effort at some thing. Hence if you really want to Xeper, conquer fear by doing something you didn't think you could. Or find a mystery and bring it to the surface of your understanding — or better yet, the understanding of others. Or create something new (the last would be an example of the verb for Create, S'Xeper). Since Xeper exists as a noun, you can interact with the Xeper of others— you are affected (usually blindly) by the Work of past magicians, or if you have learned the art of Shaping and Seeking your own Xeper **first** you can consciously Work with other's products.

I'll leave you with one other word for your word-hoard— the dual noun Xeperi. Egyptian nouns can be singular (one cat), dual (two cats), or plural (too many cats). The noun Xeperi can best be translated by synchronicity; although the standard translation is *miracle*. The Egyptians knew the Sign of something Coming Into Being was the meaningful coincidence. We know too— either by Shu ("What were the odds of that happening?") or by Tefnut ("It sent shivers down my spine."). The noun Xeperi shows that manifestations are not continuous, but discrete — actions at a distance — or more simply, magic. Xeper has occurred when two discrete systems resonate with one another. Another form of Xeperi is that moment of communication of wordless magical information with one another. The most familiar form of this is through our interactions with the Aeon, and, as before, the more adept you are at Seeking and Shaping your own Xeper, the more you can positively interact with the Xeper of the Aeon, and help fulfill her purpose of exporting Xeper into the Objective Universe.

Think about these things. Think about them till that shiver runs down your back. Then put this aside for awhile and come back to it. Then, after the most personal and individual of experimentation you too can Know and Heed the Law: Xepera Xeper Xeperu = I Have Come Into Being, and by the Process of my Coming Into Being, the Process of Coming Into Being is Established.

I will speak on the Word's history, and I will ask you all to think on this Evolution in the objective universe, and then upon the Evolution of your own subjective universe— how you, the reader, has experienced Xeper. With each evolution of the Word, note how it doesn't lose meaning, but gains through each historical text— just as Xeper in your self gains as you gain new being.

The formula "Xepera Xeper Xeperu" has been traced by French Egyptologists back to the First Intermediate period. There it was a formula of power for finding meaning when the Divine Kingship, the most important source of order, had collapsed. This was probably the birth of the Left Hand Path — the idea that meaning can only come from the individual. "Xeper" was the last fortress — the mind and body of the individual. "Xeper" was the word of anyone who would not let the divine principle of Isolation and Evolution fail.

The second appearance was in Ramses III's time. The formula was used to empower travelers through the desert. "Xeper" was a touchstone for those who extend existence by passing boundaries. "Xeper" was the word of the extender of Egypt— of the Known Order.

The third appearance was at the beginning of the Hermetic tradition. "Xeper" became the word of the individual magician seeking two types of power: power to see through the illusions of this world, and power for a coherent afterlife. These practitioners began a magical practice that went beyond the state goals of Egypt or Greece or Rome.

The fourth appearance — connected with the purchase of Budge's *Egyptian Language* by a Priest of Mendes — was very different. The Left Hand Path was up and running. The Word Worked on a matrix of its own making. Michael Aquino had to find the word (cast in Roman and Greek letters) in a translation from its last appearance. He didn't write the Rhind papyrus, any more than its author came up with the spell of Continuous Re-Creation. But his Utterance of that Word — in a matrix conditioned by its last appearance — produced a new access to energy and power beyond any previous utterances. Aquino's Utterance in 1975 e.v. was the Utterance of the Word of Aeons, defining the process that each sapient being must experience in order to change him- or herself.

Xeper is the concept upon which the cycles of manifestation are actualized (in both the noumenological and phenomenological worlds). The actual activity of cyclical dynamism is generated by the formula of Xepera Xeper Xeperu, and my Remanifestation of the Word with my own Utterance of Xeper on the Spring Equinox of 1996 e.v. will raise and attune the imagination of the world to a new and permanent understanding of the principle.

My Utterance of the Word is in the tradition of Michael Aquino's. I am Uttering the Word into a Matrix of its own conditioning. The results should be stronger and further reaching than Michael Aquino's Utterance — just as he or she that follows me will extend the Word further.

Each Pharaoh attempted to extend the borders of the country further than his predecessor. I am extending the possibilities for Xeper further than Michael Aquino. My accomplishments will be less, the time of seeing an Aeon being born is very rare. My job will be to find and articulate more of the properties of Xeper, so that each student of the Black Arts will have new **types** of tools for their collaboration with Set.

If I manage to extend the boundaries and make there my Oath of Truth, then I will be seen as a successful Magus. If I fail, others will Utter "Xeper," just as mankind has been doing for the last four thousand years. It is the job of the Temple to keep the connections of the Word alive, so that long periods of ignorance come not again. In fact, if we fail utterly then the Word will not be heard on this earth again.

The beginning Work of the Left Hand Path initiate is to learn the formula, Xepera Xeper Xeperu, which is rendered in English as "I Have Come Into Being, and by the Process of my Coming Into Being, the Process of Coming Into Being is Established." Not learning the formula as a mantra, but learning to see its effects in your life. Learn to see your Xeper as the one Truth that separates you from the mass of delusions that we create in our minds so that we might sleep-walk through existence. Having learned to awaken to the Reality of Xeper, learn to ask yourself where you wish to steer — "What do I want to do?" "What do I want to Become?" and then thirdly act accordingly — while keeping that divine realization fresh in your mind and soul.

Questions for your meditations. Remember these are only starting points.

What Principle would be worth organizing an artificial life around? Who do I know that deserves my Love? How often do I fail in giving it? If I were to make a world (as an exercise of sheer imagination) what would it be like? What would I need to do to myself to make myself as brave as Gurdjieff facing the Bolsheviks? What mass social movements are coming into being right now, that are the exact opposite of I stand for— magically and philosophically? If I had to create a pantheon of gods — a trickster, a creator, a love god or goddess, and so forth — what would I create? How do those choices tell me that I am another's creation, while at the same time seeking to both become Self-Created and a Creator in my own right? What people have I known that I would call Creators? Why? How does observing the act of Creation both establish and limit yourself? What things have I created in my life? Did any of them take on 'a life of their own'?

Magical Tasks. During this session you have three tasks. One is to talk to everyone in your life about what a "world" is — what do they mean when they say someone lives on "another planet," or if they refer to the "world of Thomas Jefferson" or the "world of a martial artist." You should likewise look up the etymologies of the words "World," "Eon," "Age," "Gaia," and "Realm." Write these etymologies down in your magical diary as well as any thoughts they may produce. Your second task is to travel to the highest point you can in your vicinity, and spend some time looking down on the landscape. The best way to do this would be to leave work, put on your best clothes, and travel to the highest office building downtown. Have tea in the top floor restaurant in the afternoon, looking down at the world, while making your diary entries for that day. During the week, read everything you can about the life of Gurdjieff and/or read all the Creation myths you can. You must also re-read the CHAOS section of your diary just before you do the ritual.

The third task is to brew a quantity of hydromel and drink a swig of it after each utterance of the Day-Taking and Night-Taking phrase. You will also drink some during the Rite. The remaining hydromel can be given to your friends. It will increase their poetic gifts and heal the sick.

Here is the process of brewing the hydromel.

Combine two pints of organic honey from your region, two pints of especially pure water, and two pints of milk. While you are whisking these things together, say the following charm five times:

"Wisdom is Sweet, and Inspiration is the most valued of all things. The Sarmouni gathered honey from all cultures. It was mead in the North and Soma in the East. It was the Secret of the Amethyst charm of the Greeks. The great god of the Left Hand Path Aristaios taught mankind the art of beekeeping that we might Remember the taste of Wisdom, and our friend the Bee stings us awake when we sleep as did Telepinus. Sweet is the taste of Wisdom that reminds us to fashion our own Creation, my father Bolverker knew its worth."

You will wish to keep the mixture refrigerated.

The Ritual
Opening. Say the word "Ohh" in a deep vibratory manner nine times.

"Here is the myth that world told me. There is naught of me that is of me. All I am and will be and have been is the work of other gods. Some called them Yahweh, some call them the Big Bang, some call them the Goddess. This is a lie. I reject it!"

Symbolically destroy a copy of the creation myth you once wholly believed in— Genesis, or Origin of the Species. After you have destroyed the myth, say the following words, filling in the gender references and names.

"I existed as I in the far-off Primal Time. From that sacred time, my Will moved to the Realm of Chaos, my Spirit moved upon the waters, my Thought incarnated through the spiral strands of DNA. Let all the Cosmos, hear now my Bon echoing in the world of Chaos from my Spell that incarnated me,

"I am Ye-gshen-dbang-rdzogs, the Primal Priest of Perfect Power, and I fashion a (man/woman) giving him/her the Name of Wer-Ma Nyi-nya, Great Hero. He/She has the head of a lion, and the ears of a lynx, a fierce face and an elephant's nose, a crocodile's mouth and a tiger's fangs, feet like swords, and feathers like sabers, and upon his hornless brow is a wish-granting gem."

Hold up the hand mirror and look upon your physical form.

"He/she will erect the Temples of five trihedrons unto the Daemons of Creation that made his body and filled his mind, for they serve my Will, and the Will of the Prince of Darkness, but his/her mind, body and actions shall be a Temple unto me, a Secret place of power that cultivates what I may yet be. His/her name shall be (your full birth name).

"Thus I Spoke in the far-off Primal Time. Speech without words, for I am the Nameless god, who quests for his own Name through Creation. All Power comes from Quest, and the way for my Quest was opened by my Primal *Bon*.

"I take now the experience of my actions in the world, both in this and other states before this, and by experiencing it now, reaffirm my first Invocation."

Drink deeply of the hydromel.

"At this moment, Heka is my Name, Magic is my Name, and by this Name in the here and now, I accept responsibly for each of my actions. I will Create myself day by day, and what I Create shall change all of the Cosmos after the manner of my Creation. I am known as Xepera, the Self-Created God. All other gods express some of what I might be, and I Created them as clues to where I must develop myself in the fullness of Time.

"In my divine wisdom I chose this time and place, I marked this body with my *Naugal*. I gave myself the fuel for the Eternal Flame, and now if I can ignite it with Intent, I will burn forever as a Star in the Heavens, looking down on the world of Chaos and ruling as a Sign of the Zodiac."

Closing. Strike your chest nine times in a Victorious manner, to remind you that Victory must be gained here and now. Each time you strike your chest cry out, "Oh!" Write up your impressions in your diary, and then read about the next session.

INCUBATION

The instructions for this session are different than those that have gone before.

Write the word INCUBATION in your diary. Beneath it write the letter "E" in a circle, just as you have written the other letters.

Put your diary away.

This session, be sure to either give away the remaining hydromel to friends or family who might need it (tell them it's a health drink), or pour it onto fertile ground.

This session you should return to your ordinary life. Watch lots of TV, avoid novel situations, surf the 'Net. If you find yourself thinking about Initiation, push the thought from your mind, distract yourself somehow.

You should live as you normally do with three exceptions:

1. Do not practice any magic of any kind at all— especially Divination to "see how you're doing." If you fail in this, you will have to start again.

2. Do not tell anyone about your experiences so far.

3. If you normally keep a diary, don't. There should be no records of this session.

In short try to live your life as much as you think you would without the Quest to Become a Lord of the Left Hand Path.

On the ninth night, read about the next session.

BIRTH

First write the word BIRTH in your diary. The letter for this session is "T."

The Day-Taking phrase is "I am Sophia-Prunikos, who rises above her condition by Grace from her Core-Self. I am Sophia. I am Hourea. I am Barbelo. All gods desire me, but I resist them all. My coming ends their hegemony!"

The Night-Taking phrase is "I am Set, who rises from death and adversity ever-stronger. I am Bata. I am Erbeth. I am the god of the feeling of Resistance being overcome. I am Ogun, I bring the ruin of symmetry."

The essay for Birth follows.

During the last nine days, you experienced flashes of the Mystery of Birth. It feels like Clarity. It is that power that comes back to you when you are deeply asleep and awakens you to action. All of our lives we will engage in things that we deem Good for us, maybe it's reading, maybe it's calling an old friend we knew since grade school, but somehow or other we just stopped. Maybe we felt bad about it. Maybe we intended to do the practice again.

Then one day, without any prior thought, we just did it again. Suddenly without *conscious intervention*, we did what we used to do, and wanted to do. This is the mystery of Birth. It is rare, hoped for, and to be encouraged. This state will take you back to the Left Hand Path. Now you will fall off the Path, it is against the grain of the world, and as such the world wins from time to time. Let us look at an examination of this state by William James as quoted by William Atkinson in *The Will* (1915):

> Desire, wish, will are states of mind which everyone knows, and which no definition can make plainer. We desire to feel, to have, to do, all sorts of things which at the moment are not felt, had or done. If with the desire goes a sense that attainment is not possible, we simply *wish*; but if we believe that the end is in our power, we *will* that the desired feeling, having, or doing shall be real; and real it presently becomes, either immediately upon the willing or after certain preliminaries have been fulfilled.... We know what it is to get out of bed on a freezing morning in a room without a fire, and how the very vital principle within us protests against the ordeal. Probably most persons have lain on certain mornings for an hour at a time unable to brace themselves to the resolve. We think how late we shall be, how the duties of the day will suffer; we say 'I *must* get up: this is ignominious' etc., but still the warm couch feels too delicious, the cold outside too cruel, and the resolution faints away and postpones itself again and again just as it seemed on the verge of bursting the resistance and passing over into the decisive act. Now how do we *ever* get up under such circumstances? If I may generalize from my own experience, we more often than not get up without any struggle or decision at all. We suddenly find that we *have* got up. A fortunate lapse of consciousness occurs; we forget

both the warmth and the cold; we fall into some reverie connected with the day's life, in the course of which the idea flashes across us, 'Hello! I must lie here no longer' — an idea which at that lucky instant awakens no contradictory or paralyzing suggestions, and consequently produces immediately its appropriate motor effect. It was our acute consciousness of both the warmth and the cold during the period of struggle, which paralyzed our activity then and kept our idea of rising in the condition of *wish* and not of *will*. The moment these inhibitory ideas ceased, the original idea exerted its effect.

This remarkable passage illustrates the mystery of Birth. The Birth of action requires that four conditions be met. The original idea has to have been strong and connected with the firm notion that attainment is possible. Secondly, the forces preventing its achievement are of a subjective symmetric character— we have both the incentive of Sloth and the Fear of hard work. Thirdly, the Attention is drawn away from the Stasis-producing pair, and into the realm of dreams and fancy. Fourthly, once the inner world is invoked, the certainty of attainment pushes the person into action.

At this point, the Initiate has done what he needed to do. As opposed to the rationally-directed whole of his life, he has accepted that sometimes it is indeed better to "leap before looking." This bold move upsets the balance of "reasonable" forces within, and upsets the status quo without. Such an action is usually called "evil" in that it disturbs people from their slumber, or threatens such unthinking activities that have wide-scale sentimental support.

Since this is a normal human phenomenon (although much valued by the aspirants to the Black Order), it has analogs in history, as well as in your personal experience. Human history is not an ordered teleological phenomenon. However, since it arises from the actions of human beings, it chaotically reflects those actions, in partially predictable patterns. If an Initiate truly learns his or her own patterns of Becoming, he or she can sense these patterns in the movement of the world. The Left Hand Path Initiate is sharp enough to know that such patterns can not be controlled, any more than we can order the tides not to rise. But we can then decide when to launch our boats.

Likewise, since the Initiate can come to see world patterns reflecting human patterns, he or she can choose to use the ideas and thought-systems arising when various patterns are manifest in the world. If he or she is looking to re-enforce the Substance of Birth in their lives, he or she would do well to read the thinkers of the Renaissance, or of the American Revolution.

Now the phenomenon of Birth, which may be defined as the passing of an Idea into the Objective World after inaction, can be cultivated by two ways.

The first is the method of suggestion. Even when you have fallen off the path, you can still tell yourself every night as you fall asleep, "It is my destiny to be a Lord of the Left Hand Path. Doors will Open!" Just repeat that (or a similar mantra) till you doze off. If you rise during the night, do so again until you sleep. Make it into a relaxation technique to help you sleep. If your Intent was True, you will "find" yourself back on the path. (Note this human phenomenon is explained by the Right Hand Path as Grace from another entity. It is such a sacred and holy part of mankind's, they believe speaking against it to be an unforgivable sin.)

The second method is to notice how the experience felt. In even the most watered-down texts on magic (such as a book on modern management techniques) it is revealed that you can have a certain species of attainment through visualization. Picture what you want, and you will get it. That is a simple magical application of the principle of Birth. What the books don't tell you, is that if you know how something *feels* you can likewise obtain it. Mental states like enlightenment, clarity, love can be Summoned— if you have experienced them.

But the symmetry-bashing part of Birth applies in both mental and physical summonings. Once you materialize that car, it comes with a certain set of frictions and responsibilities that you will not have thought of. Once you get that flash of clarity about some situation that you're in, the bliss of ignorance will be gone. All things that come through this Seventh Doorway bring storm and stress no matter how much they are desired.

Knowing as we do the shortness of life, we grow impatient with the period of Incubation. This is as it should be. But as Initiates we also know that the period of Incubation causes frail wills to die, and badly thought-out ideas to dissolve. If it were not for the Need of Incubation all humans — even that moron neighbor of yours, yeah the one with the radio — would be magicians. What a terrible world that would be. It is good for us that our magic often will not work because of Incubation. Some people call the state "Death" or "Sleep."

The word "Birth" is to be preferred over some synonyms such as "Manifestation," "Coming Forth," "Beginning." It encodes a **very** powerful lesson for the Initiate. What comes into being this way WILL take on a life of its own. It will have your best and worst characteristics in its manifestation.

Questions for your meditations: Remember that these are only a starting point.

When have I experienced Birth? What things have I given birth to? (Make an extensive list from everything to change at your job using a Method Improvement Report to that Coven you founded while you were a Wiccan.) How do those things reflect my best and worst traits? Which of them came back and bit me in the ass? How would the world be different if we hadn't had the Middle Ages (Incubation) before the Renaissance? What former good habits of mine do I wish I would Birth again? What does it mean to be living in a world where some people are undergoing all of these different states (Incubation, Clarity, Birth, and so forth) at once? What opportunities does that offer? What dangers and frustrations does that cause? How is History tied to Initiation? How is the idea of "Birth" tied to the Wandering stage of initiation? How is it tied to the other six stages?

81

<u>Magical Tasks</u>. This session you have three tasks. First, become obsessed with physical shortcuts. Look at the buildings in your life. Can you use another door? Is there a quicker way to drive there? See how many *physical* shortcuts you can go through. Second, pay attention to the notion of physical birth. Read the birth sections of the newspaper, observe pregnant women in the news and in the world. Each time do these two meditations.

A. In a cold analytical fashion think about resources and hindrances the child is likely to have.

B. Think about what kind of genius and talent the child could have if he/she overcame those hindrances and used those resources.

C. Take some aptitude tests. Make a list of all your talents, no matter how bizarre (you can recite Basque poetry while tap-dancing?). Consider if you are using the vast wealth of resources you have, or what you might want to put in motion to set situations to use those resources.

<u>The Ritual.</u>

Opening. Say the words, "Tu Te Te Tie To Te Te Ta Ta" like a count down to a launch.

"I give thanks to the great Lady of Darkness, Hine-nui-te-po, who holds the Mystery of Incubation, who can not be pierced! Without her there can be no Magic. Without her there can be no Birth. Rûna is her Name. I am her child, and therefore Immortal."

Knock on the side of your head, as though knocking on a door. Knock seven times.

"I am the god Lugh. I am second-best at everything. I demand entrance into the overly balanced hall of the gods, so that my abundance may upset the balance. I bring ruin to symmetry."

Pick up your globe (from session number three).

"Long ago, the earth had no wobble. Every year man looked at the evening skies and said, 'All is serene and peaceful, if only I were so!' And man sat on his haunches and sighed. Then Beelzebub kicked the heavens and the Equinoxes began to progress. Man said, 'The world it is a-changin'. Don't tell the common Joe, but let's make up some stories to remind ourselves to change.' And mankind invented Priests who knew the Secret and could rule, but still things were too slow. Mithras came along, and said, 'I will toss some dirty snowballs past the planet, and that will wake them up.' And the Priests, seeing comets, said, 'Man can change himself very rapidly just as the comet streaks across the sky. Hundreds of incarnations aren't needed. Let us make a Secret Order that knows this and can rule the Priests, just as Priests rule men', and the Black Order was founded. Man remains stupid and worships comets, mistaking them for Real gods, and the Priests remain stupid and worship the stars, mistaking them for Real rulers. We alone remain to Rule, we who are the Invisible Stars of the Black Order. Great is our Rule and overpowering, when it is not obscured by the clouds of unknowing."

Put the globe down. Say the following words, and then close your eyes and perform the visualization. Do this slowly, and relax deeply, but do not fall asleep.

"The harsh laws of chance and the good fortune created by millennia of Work by the Black Order brought me here. Now I must be Born of my Hidden Self.

"I see myself floating upwards, above my body, the building, my town, my country, Earth. The sun pulls me, but I will not give my self-created light to another light, so I push outward. As I pass the planets, one by one, I feel less human, only my Essential Self remains.

"I am a Wandering Star in the blackness of space.

"I see before me the Seven Stars called the Big Dipper, or the Great Bear. Oh Arkte! I salute you! I drift toward the stars. They become doors.

"Seven harsh-looking men step from the Doors. I will be as them for a time, just as they once were as I am now. They roar barbarous names. Their enchantment falls on me. They have arranged tough but fair lessons for me in my life from which I will Learn what can not be written in books.

"Seven beautiful women step out behind the men. I will be as them for a time, just as they once were as I am now. They bless me with silvery wands. Their enchantments fall upon me. They have given me incredible luck in the world that will move into wonderful places at the most unexpected times."

The men and women enter the star doors, and close them.

"I see there is a Great Darkness behind the Stars. Something is stepping forth. It is the Prince of Darkness (He/she) looks like me. (He/she) walks to me and whispers a Great Secret in my Ear. It is for me alone. I grow faint, but I will Remember and grow Strong.

"I return now to Earth, because only there can I grow my Secret. Only there can Ideas be made Real. As I pass the planets, one by one, I feel my humanity returning, but each layer of humanity is now a garment and not a shell. The forces of history that instructed me as a child, are now childish memories— Keys to my True Self, not fetters to Chaos."

Closing. Say the words, "Ta Ta Te Te To Tie Te Te Tu" very pompously as though announcing the arrival of the Emperor.

Write your impressions in your diary, and read about the next nine nights.

RE-CREATION

Write the word RE-CREATION in your diary. The letter for this session is "D."

The Day-Taking phrase is "I am Marduk, the Lord of Pure Incantation. I make the dead live, I renew the gods. In the tempest my weapons flash, in my flames are steep mountains overthrown."

The Night-Taking phrase is "I am Odhinn, the Father of Magic. For nine nights I hung upon wind-tossed pine, whose Roots run where no man knows. Without bread or drinking horn I hung, bloodied by my own Spear, Odhinn sacrificed to Odhinn. Then I saw the Runes; screaming I took them up and fell back into the world. There I waxed and grew wise and did well, and I saw how one Word leads to another Word and one Work leads to another Work."

<u>The essay for Re-Creation follows</u>:
Re-Creation is a subtle art understood only by experience. Once experienced it can be Drawn to the Self by both magic and hard work as needed. It is to be understood on four levels: surface, medial, daemonic, and essential.

Surface. Every creation made by man and unleashed upon the world needs to be periodically re-created for two reasons: A. Since the world is resistant to the products of the mind, such products will tend toward corruption, no matter how good the original idea. B. All new ideas are made in ignorance of the facts— because many of the "facts" will only be found by doing. This means every business, every college, every Temple needs to be periodically recreated. Now this is hard for two reasons: 1) The creator may have fallen in love with his or her idea (and refuse to look at how it is unfolding in the world). There is often a great deal of power in such stubborn people, but their force leads those around them to misery, madness, and despair. 2) The maintainer of the idea is comfortable in it, and knows how uncomfortable the real world may be (see the couch example above). Those who cannot Re-Create undergo what is known in Gurdjieffian parlance as "improper crystallization" or, in the common tongue, "becoming an asshole." But the Initiate knowing that Re-Creation is Necessary to keep the Idea strong in this world, makes it his or her job to know the facts, and to look at different ways of looking at the facts. This is connected with the Principle of Order (above).

Medial. Our thoughts and feelings are largely mechanical, as you have noticed by this point of the Grand Initiation. You have no doubt learned the power of simply resisting a signal so that your thoughts and feelings don't go where you don't want them to. Now it is time to learn a great secret: you can also get your thoughts and feelings to go where you want them to, by sending a signal to yourself that has worked before. If say, you are no longer in love with your spouse, you can make yourself fall in love with them again by doing some of the same activities, making lists of things that you loved about them, and so forth. This ability to Re-Create also works on the medial level of mankind. People who can not learn this skill are usually often-divorced. Allowing this to happen is a bad thing to your Initiation because it keeps you from having a secure home to Rest your Mind in. To decide *when* to apply this skill, you need a strong sense of what is valuable in your life. This is connected to the Order Principle. If "being loved" is a value, Re-Create; if it is not, don't be trapped!

Daemonic. Magic is a way of interacting with the world. It is ultimately personal. What works for Uncle Setnakt may not work for you, what works for you may not work for Uncle Setnakt. So you have to discover what works for you. **Most magical operations won't work.** Now if you find something that does Work, you will want to Re-Create it. Some people are addicted to ritual, so they will do the same rituals year after year with no results. But the Initiate learns to gather what works best for him or her. Now Re-Creation doesn't mean doing exactly the same things over and over. It means that if a money ritual took six months to pay off in the past, the next ritual had better be done six months before you need

84

the cash. But there is a deeper level to this: as you attempt to master a type of magic, you will need to rework the ceremonies that established that type of magic. If one wants to add La Vey-style Satanism to one's repertoire, one had better rework the rituals of *The Satanic Rituals*; if one wants to master the rituals of Late Antiquity, one had better try writing on papyrus at least once, and so forth. What has Worked in the past will Work again.

Essential. Ultimately one Needs to rework the rituals that Create you. You know that human evolution has been ruled by magic, although magic of mainly an unenlightened sort. Some of your ancestors married others because of the well-cast lust spell. Some of your ancestors had cultural dominance because of the rituals they practiced at a medial level. Some of your ancestors had to flee from tyranny rather than give up their rituals. These things shaped you. Mankind shaped itself, using that part of itself that was most like the Prince of Darkness. He knows, as you will know, that if you unleash magic in the world, it eventually comes to produce what you want. The Working He began with mankind, about ten to fourteen thousand years ago, Created you. If you wish to truly own yourself, you must interact with that Working in four ways—

A. You must reWork the magic that formed you.

B. You must decide if you want to have children in this life (if you already have children you have an obligation). If you do, you must be willing to lead a life of self-sacrifice so that they may have the best education and physical training you can afford, because they are your Sendings toward the great Dark called the future.

C. You must put things in the world that increase the intelligence of mankind (*i.e.*, you must act as Lucifer, the light bringer toward others), and

D. You must try to send some of your magic into the dim past and the distant future. One of the magical Secrets is that if something old is forcefully presented to the Magician (say someone unexpectedly gives you a statue of an ancient Aztec god), it is a Symbolic herald of something that your Essential Self is about to bring into being. If you Wish to communicate with the Essential Self of another, because they are your life-partner or your magical student, you can use this method of Giving as well.

Traditions can be good things, or they can be encumbrances. The best way to assess whether accretions to, or extensions of the original idea are harmful or beneficial is to return to the Root and view the accretions or extensions in the uncompromising light of the original Principle. This is seldom done in the occult world, so vital traditions often choke on their own weeds.

Questions for your meditations: Remember that these are only a starting point.

What things have you had to Re-Create in your life? What was hard and what was fun about having to do so? How much of your sex life involves Re-Creation? (In other words, you do something because it really turned you on once.) What does that tell you about the Uses of sex magic? Why is Re-Creation so powerful in the world right now? (We're seeing all sorts

85

of Re-Created entities like the Temple of Set and the Rune-Gild.) What entities in your life Need to be Re-Created in accord with their original principles? What are some ways you can begin that Re-Creation? What magical systems of the past would you like to see Re-created? Have you ever been reading a magical or philosophical document and felt that you wrote it? What documents? Does that mean you are a Re-Creation of others? Do you feel that your daemonic self is partially a Re-Creation of others? If so, how does that relate to the sex magic question, the Re-creation in the world question, and the choice of a School of Initiation?

Magical tasks. You will have three magical tasks this session. First, reread the Order section of your diary a couple of times during the week. Second, plan a short trip to visit some place you enjoy. The ideal would be a day trip to visit a museum, or park, or restaurant you like. Feel free to travel with someone. Think about how you felt last time you were there, how you feel this time, and how you changed. Have fun. Third, look at several sketches of gargoyles, demons, satyrs, and other horned beasts. Imagine their horns as antennae, one for Creation and one for ReCreation, pouring the feelings needed for each into the world. Just have fun with this image.

The Ritual.

Prepare a square of parchment with the following figures on the front and back of it:

Reverse

12	13	4	6	148
13	9	148	12	6
4	148	8	148	33
16	23	148	9	5
148	27	4	21	31

Obverse

U	R	I	E	L
R	I	L	U	E
I	L	I	L	I
E	U	L	I	R
L	E	I	R	U

Fix it to your forehead with the numbers facing your skull and the letters facing the world.

Opening. Sing the following words, "Du Da Di De Do Ddddooo Ddddeee Dddddiiiii Ddddaaaaa." Imagine energy swirling up from the floor and swirling around you into the midpoint of your being, then spiraling outward, but rather than it passing out from your body, it concentrates in your head, beneath the parchment.

"I fashioned the world as best I knew how. From the giant's brow I made the heavens; from his molars and bones, the stones; from his sweat and blood, the oceans. But there were Secrets hidden in the giant's body, secrets I only gleaned after hard work. Each Secret lured me on like a dancer. I thought she had dropped her last veil, but another veil remained. As I Learned by chasing her, as I Learned by shaping mountains, as I Learned by digging up ancient scrolls hidden in the desert, I Knew I had to start again. Life is short, and I could not start a new life, but I could ReCreate the one I had. The day I really Understood this, one of the Illuminati came to me. 'Hail man,' he said. 'You shall wield what is called Black Magic, which ReWorks the Mysteries of the Cosmos. It is the true spawn of that great Black Flame which first brought thy Will to life long ages ago.'

"I went then to erect a Temple unto the glories of my Creation, and in the Pure Land I met the Masters of the Realm who had erected the Temples of the Eight Trihedrons unto the Hidden Sun. And as I cleared the land, they came upon me, and threw me to the sandy ground, crying out, 'Who are you that you would work in the past, the present, and the future? Say your name and show us your sign or we shall throw you to the apes who guard the gates.'

"And I rose and said my Names."

Look in the hand mirror after each Name. Imagine the Seal on your forehead to be glowing with infernal light.

"I am Uriel, the Messenger who says that Time is Past and a new Order must begin.

"I am Rilue, at whose Word ancient cites rise from the ocean depths to herald a new age.

"I am Ilili, the smith who can fashion anything, come to fix your talismans and lamps.

"I am Eulir, he that has risen up and may unleash true Magic in the world.

"I am Leiru, who is the King of the Crossroads, and the ancestor of all Path travelers.

"They did marvel at my names and draw back, but one of them still challenged me, 'What is the Sign that we might know you are our brother/sister?'"

Show the sign as you speak. Use your left hand. Extend your index and pinkie fingers. The midpoint is just above the navel. For the Shadow, reach your hand to the left as though you were resting it upon an invisible man or woman's right shoulder.

"I Touch my brow for the use of reason to tell us when to raze and rebuild. I Touch my heart for the use of feelings to know when to sing the old songs. I Touch my midpoint for the use of will to inspire the laborers who will come in my Name. I Touch the Shadow to make the stones rise up and fly through the air to the appointed site.

"He said, 'This is the Sign in its inner form. What is the Sign in its outer form?'"

Trace an inverted Pentagram in front of you. Begin with the lowest point, which should be about the height of your midpoint.

"The Masters of the Realm cheered, and said to me, 'We welcome you to the Order of Builders in the name of our Pir Thuban the Black. You are come at the appointed time. For there was an Age of Silver, and Witchcraft ruled the world; then there was an Age of Gold, and Masonry ruled the world; then there was an Age of Precious Stones of the First Water, and angular magic ruled the world; but now is come this night the Age of Ultimate Sparks of Intimate Fire, when Will alone shall rule the world. Build now your Temple and broadcast your will from it for all the ages."

Spend some time with eyes closed imagining a great pyramid being built by you towering in the desert night. When it is built, imagine a great sunrise happening, and the pyramid casting a large shadow over the tiny cities of men.

Take the Seal from your forehead.

"This is the part that Re-creates what lives beyond the fields of space and time. Men call it destiny."

Take the Seal from the rite you performed for Order.

"This is the part that Orders the fields of Space and Time. Through it Ideas are made Real. Men call it forethought.

"I unite them forever."

Burn the two seals together. Destroy the ashes.

Closing. As you sing this song, imagine the energy flowing out of your head and down to your midpoint; it swirls around there and then flows back into the world. "Ddddaaa Ddddiiii Ddddeee Ddddooo Do De Di Da Dddduuuuuuuu."

Write your impressions in your diary, and read about the next nine nights.

VICTORY

Write the word VICTORY in your diary. The letter for this session is "H."

The Day-Taking phrase is "I am (State your full birth name), who enjoys unique rewards as the result of my hard labor. Each reward is another step to Becoming an Immortal, Independent, Potent, and Powerful Essence. The hard work opens all Doors, the mysteries give it Joy, and my magic Teaches me directly."

The Night-Taking phrase is "I am (State your magical name), who Knows my Teachers, my Enemies, my Friends, and my Lovers. My mind is a wish-granting jewel. It is a Crystallizer of Dreams, through which the Black Flame casts dark rainbows of delight into all the worlds. Greater than all men am I, but much greater still is my Journey."

The essay for Victory follows:

One of the most important ideas for the Left Hand Path is that of the unique reward. If the Path deifies as its prime virtue "Individuality," then the "carrot" for going through the many rites-of-passage that you must traverse must be unique unto you. The ultimate form of that reward is not, can not, and should not be an easily definable state peculiar to the world of four dimensions and five senses. Uncle Setnakt has known magicians who have said, "I want a good car, a good lover, and a good job." Certainly laudable goals, but when achieved, they quit the Path. No Sovereignty for them.

Now this does not mean that such things are to be despised. In fact pursuing such goals are Necessary to provide you with both the motivation to continue and the friction needed to Transform your fragments of Self into a Immortal, Independent, Potent, and Powerful Essence. Along the way you must set your goal posts. Now a womanizing Egyptologist might have as a goal post making love to women in a newly discovered tomb on the night of his fortieth birthday. His reward might be different than the country music fan that gets to sing with her favorite artist on an album. Neither of them would be very happy with the reward of the computer scientist who gets to perform statistical analysis on the biggest intranet in the Western world.

Now when we achieve these goals, we Need to do four things. Firstly, we must pause and remind ourselves how much sweeter these goals are because of our Struggle to get them. That is basic human psychology. But we must see that sweetness as the same sweetness that the hydromel represented as it passed our palate. Secondly, we must realize how the reward contained the other steps — how it contained the Chaos of the world, our sense of Order, our Clarity, and so forth — because we are about to embark on that Cycle again, and we want to do so with greater Knowledge. Thirdly, we must savor the reward because it points to what our next type of Being could be. It is an indicator of where we might go with our evolution both in this life and the next. Fourthly, we must realize that the Seed from this experience did not come from Chaos, but from the "Idea" of Victory, herself.

Consider your path through the first eight sessions. Now I know that some of my readers didn't do the Work, all they did was read sections of the Rituals aloud (or silently if they feared it might bother their roommates in their dinky little apartments). That is as Real as pinning on a round piece of yellow plastic after watching someone win a gold medal at the Olympics. But for those few of you who have gone the distance and done the work, consider your path.

At first it was easy, because of the bloom of novelty. But some days were very hard. Suddenly Life seemed committed to stop you. Then it was boring and you missed watching television. Then you began to wonder if maybe I was simply having fun with you — maybe I just made it all up —

maybe I've never done a ritual in my life. Then you had the days when Revelation hit so hard and fast, that you worried if your head would explode. Then there was a night or two when you were just plain scared — was that a ghost you heard? Someone breaking into your house? Then you were depressed. Then there were days when you could barely even go through the motions. Then there were days when you were crazy, you were expecting to meet me on the street, or you were sure that your landlord was one of the Illuminati.

But you continued. You began to really Learn some hard Truths about yourself, and you begin to have stirrings of other types of consciousness or the awakening of occult powers.

Then you wondered if other people had had the same effects. Of if you were alone. Then you realized that there are whole classes of internal phenomena that you will never be able to share with anyone. You are Alone. And if you can't hack that, you can not precede along the Path.

Now you are coming to the end of the Grand Initiation. You're relieved and you're scared. You're scared because you have timed this to be over just as some important life event begins. Maybe you're going to start graduate school. Maybe it's your thirtieth birthday. Maybe you're about to move to Australia. Maybe you're getting that sex change operation.

And you prepared for it, using self knowledge and magic.

Are you a nut?

Sure, many people will say so. But you are an Initiate, you have Knowledge of yourself, secret powerful knowledge that you wrote out with your own hand. It didn't come from me, it came from that guy or gal in the mirror you've been seeing at least twice a day.

Some of you will go very, very far with this start.

Some will be minor magicians that are— pretty good plumbers, let's say.

All will have an immunity to curses as long as they are true to themselves, all will draw magical influences to aid them wherever they go, all will have mysteries appear before them (although it will be their hard work to seek after these mysteries), all will have the same sort of disasters that normal folk do— but they will have the ability to use the bad circumstance to wake themselves up, all will be just a little bit luckier than their fellows. You will have made a Pact with yourselves.

I mentioned the idea of the magical name above. As you grasped in the fifth section, the Left Hand Path magician leads an artificial life to counter the primary weakness of his or her being. One of the greatest aids for this life is to choose a magical name that sums up the *method* you wish to use to obtain. Some people choose the name of gods, which I feel is a bad practice since it may make you think that you have *already* obtained your goal. I suggest picking the Name of a heroic figure that Resonates with the type of unique reward that you want. If you love Stonehenge, and you use the Ogham as a divinatory tool, you might take a name like Merlin. If you love the idea of pacts with the Devil and the sinister glamour of Satanism, Faust has much to recommend it. If you love to find your way out of complex situations and you like really hot sex, Adrian will do. If you decide to choose a divine name, pick a god or goddess that had to *do* something to achieve their status.

Once you have picked the name (and you can change these— but like dating don't do it too much), you should gather such things as remind you of the Name. You should research its origins and give yourself gifts of art and clothing that reflect the experience.

At first your magical name won't mean much. But it can come to inform you, and even be a Source of magical power.

That leads me to the question of the magical names I've constructed these rituals with. Some are going to be super familiar, others are pretty difficult to find. This is intentional. I would guess that with the exception of scholars in the field of comparative religion, no one will recognize all the names. This is in part to give you a sense of mystery, but also to give you a special *frisson* when you do encounter the names. The names have been drawn from a wide range including Toltec, Norse, Maori, Aztec, Tibetan, Greek, Etruscan, Navaho, Hebrew, Persian, Babylonian, Egyptian, Roman, Gnostic, Celtic, and other sources like *The Sacred Magic of Abra-Melin the Mage*. Some of the symbolism is fairly easy to understand, such as the little birthday cake in the fourth section; other parts are a bit arcane, such as the reworking of the Mithras Liturgy in the seventh section. This will give you many magical leads over the next few years. However I will assure you that they are not randomly drawn together. Each is an exemplary archetype of the forces you are seeking to Invoke in yourself, Recognize in your past actions, Utilize for self creation, and Direct in the outer world for Rulership.

<u>Questions for your meditations</u>. Remember that these are just starting points.

What have been the best moments of your life? What did each of these special moments lead to? What would be your best fantasy job? Your sex fantasy? How can you work to make these things real? If you could be any god you wanted to, who would you pick and why? What self-realization that you have had during this Initiation surprised you most? What would your favorite god (see question before) do about that? What special powers do you feel you have shown at times of Victory? (For example, telepathy during great sex.) What would be a rational training program to try and make that power part of your daily life? How do your actions set up for Victories of another? How have the actions of others in the past set up for your Victories?

<u>Magical Tasks</u>. You must come up with three magical tasks for you to do this session that Symbolize your understanding of the idea of Victory. The first must be the hardest job you do during the Grand Initiation. The second must be an outrageous display of hedonism sometimes toward the middle of these nine nights. The third must be something that was inspired by your dreams during the Grand Initiation.

<u>The Ritual</u>

You must begin naked. You will put on the clothes that you removed at the beginning of the Grand Initiation after the end of the rite. You must have a main altar and a secondary altar set up as in the first rite. You will begin at the main altar, then work at the secondary, then walk to your clothes.

Opening. In a very breathy voice say, "HHHH HHHHH HHHHH HHHHH HHHHH HHHUUUU HHHHAAA HHHHOOOO HHHUUUUMMM!"

"I have traveled through the Nine Pylons. I have journeyed though the Nine Angles. I have traversed the Nine Knots. I have voyaged through the Nine Dimensions. I will now unify my forces and Become the magician I have always longed to be."

Light a Black candle.

"Hail the Black Flame, Symbol of the Prince of Darkness's only Gift to me! It blazeth in brilliance and darkness unto the beginning and ending of dimensions unto Glory of Desire! I Bless the Prince of Darkness with such magic as I might possess, and Vow from my Essential Self to Become a fit companion for Him someday."

Place your left hand over your heart.

"Hail the thoughts and feelings that mankind has developed through their striving. Hail the myths and art that bring these feelings to me. I Swear from my Medial Self that I will Send into the world things of beauty and thought to Awaken others and give them Joy. By my Vision and my Voice shall I send the Black Flame across the expanses of Space and Time."

Run your hands over your body.

"Hail the rich experience of being Alive in the Here-and-Now that Centers and Informs me. Hail the pleasures and pains of existence that provide me with all I truly Need! I Affirm with my Surface Self that I will Awaken, See, and Act in Here-and-Now. I am alive, and grow more alive each passing Night."

Reach both hands over the altar as if beckoning someone.

"I call my Daemonic self, which has wandered through all places of magic since I began this Rite. I long for Thee, to Know the Secrets that you will whisper to me. Come now, oh my fetch, and be one with me! Speak now, oh my Daemon, that I may know of all things! Spin me, oh my ally, that I may be more than human! Converse with me, my Holy Guardian Angel, that I may enliven all the material I have written and thought this last eighty-one nights. You gave your eye to Mimir and Drank of his Well. You enchanted the Sand Dune boy and he let you pass where no human has trod. You sang the serpents to Sleep and stole the Golden Fleece. You surprised Lao Tzu and stole from him the Peach of Immortality. Be now One with me!"

Feel the daemon returning to you.

"I yoke myself to my Daemonic Self that I shall become a master of magic, and travel through all lands, now that locks spring open at my word, and faery realms show themselves plainly to me. I will travel far and be transformed thereby! When I die it will live in the Earth— as an act of Love, I will it to aid another traveler on the *via sinistra*!"

Now turn your back on the main altar and walk to the smaller one. Drink a sweet drink from the goblet you have placed there.

"I have tasted Victory, and in her sweet taste I have tasted Chaos, Order, Clarity, Life, Creation, Incubation, Birth, Re-Creation, and my own hidden Name. By returning to my source I have united the four levels of my being, and each Night hence the world becomes more and more the variable and I the Constant."

Turn to face the West.

"I will Know my Enemies, and I will take from them their magic, their wisdom, and their wealth, if they have not the sense to flee me."

Turn to face the South.

"I will Know my lovers, and I will honor and cherish them, and I will sacrifice my foolish ego for their support, lessons, and love."

Turn to face the East.

"I will Know my friends, and I will Strive to Know their ambitions and harmonize them with my own."

Turn to face the North.

"I will Know my Teachers, and I will Strive to Learn all they can Teach, and profit from the trials both they and Life set for me. I will Bless their names, and my magic will support their work:

"I send my magic tonight to bless all that have Taught me by Word or Deed. I receive this night the blessing of all those whom I will Teach. I send this night my magic to bless all who labored to bring me into the world, to raise me, to feed me. I receive this night all of their good wishes, which I did not understand, but which now feed my soul as their food fed my body. I send my magic to Awaken others who are born into this Age to ally with me in the fashioning of great deeds. I receive this night subtle signals that will guide my steps to be in the right place to work on great projects to reshape the world. I send this night my magic to bless the ripples my lifeline will Create so that it may set in motion wonders for those who come after me. I receive this night the benefit of magical tides Created by those of the Black Order so that my boat may reach its port sooner!

"So it is Done and so it shall Be!"

Walk to your old clothes that you put aside so long ago. Put them on and face away from the altar. Picture a Black Pillar to your right, and a White Pillar to your left.

"On my left is the effect the Black Order always has upon the world. Hated as revolutionaries and blasphemers, their work blesses the world. On my right is the absolute and eternal need for Work, it is the pillar that says every morning, 'What is the Work for today?'

"The sky is held up by four pillars."

Closing. In a very vibratory voice say, "HHHH HHHH HHHH HHHH HHHH HHHUUUU HHHHAAA HHHHOOOOO HHHHHUUUUUMMMM!"

Now write up your impression of the rite, and anything else you wish to add. When you feel that you are done, write down the three rows of seven letters and the three numbers that appear at the end of this book. Put your diary away and clean up the area. Soon you will be very busy in the new life event, plus trying to do the nineteen methods of practice outlined in chapter two of this book. For magical fun, you can try to track down the names in these sections, and get the goodies in the resource section. This will keep you busy, and it will provide you with a great deal of material on all four levels of dynamism to process. After nine months, you should take out your diary and read it. It will provide you with inspiration in many ways. Perhaps you can start working out the cipher of the letters and numbers; much wisdom is contained there.

You may copy out ideas from your diary for other magicians, but do not let them read it while you live. After your death you should will it, along with your magical estate, to another magician, and then they can read it. It will be a special boost for them, as well as giving you power to act in this world, if you so desire.

Chapter Four

Resources

This chapter has four sections and one lesson. Let's do the lesson first, then look at the sections.

Everything in your life is a Resource. Because of the profound sleep that mankind has, we don't see this. In fact the greatest power against our Becoming a Lord of the Left Hand Path is the fact we don't know what our resources are.

We ignore them again and again, and we put off starting things in the belief that what we really Need is outside of our lives.

Let's consider the path of a certain young sorceress I know. (No, this is not about my wife and I— although our story is very magical.) Early in her life she had a great deal of emotional hurt, in fact a truly sorry sonafabitch tried to rape her. Other men took advantage of her in emotional and financial ways, and she fell deeply asleep, working in low-paying boring jobs in environments that were unhealthy on several levels. But she never fell completely asleep; she continued to have great luck in materializing material goods, especially books. This gave her an uncritical interest in the occult.

Her little home was full of books. I'm talking thousands of volumes. Everything from rare and precious grimoires to anthropological texts (often the best thing to study) to cheap pseudoscience paperbacks. Since she could cause these books to materialize very cheaply, she continued to be interested in the occult, but never fully felt that she could "do it." Indeed the walls of her house became like herself, thick with insulation that kept the hurtful forces of the world at bay.

Now it came to pass that she became known as something of an expert on occult topics. She did nothing to further this rumor, but every used bookstore clerk in a hundred miles of her home had seen her buy up books on magic like there was no tomorrow. So they pointed her out to various seekers.

One of these was a young materialistic warlock of a rather immature school of the Left Hand Path. He tried to get her acquaintance. Needless to say she was very shy, and had very strong boundaries— like the Great Wall of China. But he persisted, and in the process fell quite in love with her. He used all of his skills to make their time enchanting, and she fell in love with him.

He introduced her to the virtues of magical Selfishness. She decided to try to work magic for certain aims rather than for more books. At first it backfired every time. Every ritual meant the loss of a job, or of health, or of an old friend. Her Need increased, and there was a great danger of her going completely back into her shell for good. The young warlock was very sad, but he was not far enough along the path to be able to do anything except give her quick fixes. (He was at the second level of Sovereignty, the Quest for Strength.) But she persevered long enough to do a big ritual asking for a Guide.

Then everything went quiet in her life. Magic stopped being an interest, and she did start doing some practical things like learning word processing skills, and exploring job aptitudes. Her life-partner studied her books and worked on his magic craft, saddened that his partner was not part of that part of his life, but gladdened that she was out of the spiral of disaster.

Then a set of circumstances brought him to a more mature School of the Left Hand Path. His slow but steady progress through the Path became much, much more solid when he was able to rest upon a firm intellectual base. His Teacher visited him to perform certain rites to insure the School's growth in his area. By "accident" the Teacher's car broke down at a flea market she had taken him to. So the Teacher had to spend several hours with her, waiting for a tow truck that kept getting later and later. She told the Teacher about her life— she hadn't really meant to do this, but real Teachers have this effect on people. He saw that her problem was self image. She equated herself with the truly crappy way people treated her. He offered some suggestions — mainly couched in the sort of occult ideas she was familiar with — of magical ways to improve her self image.

After many hours, she had decided to join the Teacher's School. He went back to his car, tried it, and it started up just fine as the tow truck finally rolled in.

She had a very hard go of it at first, she was so full of the collected "occult wisdom" of her vast library, but as soon as she changed her self image, things started to change.

She looked around her community for free classes on writing resumes and getting jobs. She made an inventory of the skills she had picked up in the many jobs she had worked in. She used her sorcery to get a car, so that she could drive to interviews in a nearby metropolis. She volunteered her skills to the Teacher to help put out some of his writings, and in the process she began to learn how to tell a good book from a bad book.

She had lots of bad books.

She got better jobs. She lost some weight, got a make-over, and put her money into a wardrobe instead of books.

She got jobs doing what she liked. She liked to use layout skills, she liked to teach new employees, she liked to deal with the public in short intense bursts.

She opened a part-time occult bookstore. After all she had thousands of books to sell.

She and her life partner were able to take some trips around the world. (She didn't sell the books as cheaply as she had bought them.)

She began making contacts with the occult community around the world, so she and her husband had people to show them Berlin, London, Sydney.

She began Teaching with the School.

She has opened Doors for others, and some (like her) were strong enough to walk through.

She has learned how to barter her books for occult art and objects of great value.

Her home is a showcase, a Temple.

She is now midway through her life. Many people, like her, like to practice Egyptian magic. Few fly to Egypt to do so. . .

Now she has taken all the aspects of her life and made them resources. From her hurt she learned to be self-reliant. From being deceived she learned to test things on her own. From her magic she learned that things are possible. From her persistence she learned that change is hard. From the books she gathered, she assembled one of the best occult libraries on the Gulf Coast. She also gained a valuable resource that she has turned into money, art, and friends around the globe. From her husband, she got access to the School that clarified things for her. From her kazillion little no-money jobs she got a suite of skills that make her employable for good money, pretty much anywhere. From her apprenticeship to her Teacher she learned discretion and the need for creating an artificial life. She took her body and remade it into a healthy and attractive body, which is a powerful combo in today's sexist world. She transformed her house from a book storage facility into a palace that magicians from far away have traveled to see.

She didn't win a lottery, get an inheritance, or get any help. The Teacher Did nothing for her. She didn't have special training from expensive schools. She wasn't an athlete or drop-dead gorgeous. She simply used what she had. She Awakened to possibilities. The above changes took about seven years of hard Work; now she is in her early forties, and the world is her oyster. Her genes say that she will live another forty years, baring hazard. I've met her elderly relatives, they still have their wits about them, so very much will come from this person. That is the lesson of resources.

The chapter has four sections: Uncle Setnakt's Handy Oracle; Uncle Setnakt's FAQ; Some Books, Films and Tapes; and a description of the Temple of Set. Each has a use.

Uncle Setnakt's Handy Oracle will help you get through life problems in a way that gives you pointers to the Left Hand Path. Eventually you will want to seek and master a somewhat more complex divination system, but this one will give you a jump start in learning how to divine, how to use life experience to stimulate LHP thinking, and how to achieve real power in the world.

Uncle Setnakt's FAQ will help you answer some of the questions your friends and family may have about the Left Hand Path. Later as you gain your experience from practice, you will not only be able to answer these questions by yourself, but will be able to give much more thoughtful answers than Uncle Setnakt. (And unless I've missed my guess, *you* have some of these questions yourself.)

Some books, films, and tapes is a supplement to this book to help your magical and philosophical self-training. Your own experience plus the information gained in the books will tell you where to go next. This resource list is written in 1998, and will date as all such things do. Over the years you will come up with a better list. You might even take it as an exercise to think what 19 books, films, and tapes you would recommend after you have been on the Path 19 years.

The Temple of Set is the School that Uncle Setnakt gained a good deal of his training in. As of the writing of this book, he has been a member for nine years, beginning as a First Degree and penning these lines as a Fifth Degree and the High Priest of the Temple. Although this book is designed to supplement any Left Hand Path School, it is most resonant with the School that clarified my own Awakening.

Uncle Setnakt's Handy Oracle

The following Oracle will get you out of many problems, if its wise advice is heeded. However only a fool would think that all of life's questions have a mere fifteen answers. To consult the Oracle, take three six-sided dice in your left hand. Think deeply about the problem. While you roll the dice, say the four charms (this is similar to the remarks on the Tarot above):

1. In the next few hours, I will see what I have overlooked.
2. I will Learn from this situation.
3. I will See how my own actions contributed to the problem.
4. The outcome of this situation will aid me in Creating a strong inner self, and changing the outer world in accordance with my will. My Will touches the world now!

Toss the dice. You will get a number between 3 and 18. Look up the answer below. After you have contemplated how the answer might be applied, think of a plan of action. Ask the dice where that plan might need to be strengthened and toss again. Record the results in your diary (Problem, Initial Reading, Plan, Second Reading, Revised Plan, and Results).

3. Accept friction from a jerk that is teaching you useful things. Learning patience is an extra payoff.
4. Avoid bad alliances. Even leeches expect to be paid.
5. You've been through worse. This is easy if you Remember your lessons.
6. Take a mini-vacation from your woes. When you're free of worries, do a ritual that attracts wealth, wisdom, fame, and justice. Then plunge back into the fray.
7. How do the minor players in the current situation see things?
8. To achieve change, focus deeply on one thing at a time.
9. Don't play their game, but above all **don't** play your old games!
10. Stop telling everyone what a shit you are. Speak as though you already possessed the good qualities you need.
11. Gossip is the coin of the weak.
12 Share what you know and your power will grow.
13. Sleep, diet, exercise, and taking up an unexpected offer or opportunity should be at the top of your "to do" list.
14. Are your worries **your** worries? "Co-dependence" is a weapon of the forces of stupidity.

15. Think about what you have been handed recently. It is a Gift from yourSelf to yourself.

16. Assume that you are also part hypocrite and part fool. Self righteousness is most dangerous to the righteous. Better read this again.

17. Awareness **is** restful; faking something is fatiguing.

18. You have forgotten your real goals, and suddenly your life seems busy and you feel sick.

Uncle Setnakt's FAQ

Q. If the only Gift the Prince of Darkness gave us was a Model for our Becoming, why do we Invoke Him during rituals?

A. The Model of the Self we could be exists not only deep within us as our Essential (or Core) selves, but is also active in the Cosmos. We can experience the feel of that Model directly, by Invocation. This helps us examine what is strong and weak in ourselves. Each Invocation is a returning to the Root of human consciousness, and as such makes us aware of the accretions to that Principle. We can from that awareness decide which accretions further our unique Self perception, and which cloud and distort it. As we lose bad perception, such Invocations of the Prince of Darkness can begin to inform our soul directly.

Q. I met a group of teenagers that say they are LHP, but they pray to Satan, and I know a nominally Christian group that practices magic. Are either of these groups LHP?

A. Nope. Teenagers shouldn't really be on any religious path, because they have other life issues to deal with. The LHP is a philosophical and magical discipline, not an excuse to wear ragged black T-shirts. The "Christian" group wants the best of both worlds— the "Thy Will be done!" of the RHP and the "My Will be done!" of the LHP. They will piously explain how both are possible. This lets them off the hook for making decisions, and gives them a good excuse if their magic fails.

Q. If the LHP is so great, why isn't everybody on it?

A. It is too great a strain for most people. Frankly the same is true of the RHP. Things that require work aren't popular. Heck, I don't like work anymore than anyone else, and buy a lottery ticket every couple of months to try to get out of it. Most people who try their hands at the LHP find it very exhilarating at first — after all you've got magic rituals, a chance to play the bad guy and shock your pious friends, and the possibility of becoming a god — who wouldn't want that? But when faced with the idea that there is work to do, the rose disappears and only the thorns remain. If that wasn't hard enough, seeing your friends turn back isn't exactly an easy thing. The necessary cultivation of an inner solitude, when your activities will take you further and further away from the world of regular human standards and expectations, is very tough.

Q. I've spent my life picking up another belief system, can't I keep it more-or-less intact and still be LHP?

A. I've spent my life speaking English. Do I really have to learn Swedish, or can I just make my English sound Swedish? The Need to learn is great. You must put your other belief aside. Then later you can analyze it with the tools gained in LHP studies, and take from it what you Need. There was something there that appealed to your soul, or it would not have called you. But simply adding a *soupcon* of LHP thinking to an existing belief structure helps neither the belief structure nor the LHP.

Q. I know that you are the High Priest of the Temple of Set. Isn't all of your insistence on a School a thinly disguised attempt to get more Setians?
A. It is not a disguised attempt at all. I hope the smarter people who read this book and have success with some of the practices in the second chapter, are sending off for the Information letter today. But that not withstanding, a School is Necessary. It alone can provide two things for the Initiate:
1. It can show them examples that the philosophy works. Unless there is a concrete example of attainment, you will never be able to focus your Will toward your goals, and the forces of stupidity that rule the medial level of the world will form an impenetrable boundary for your development— a magical glass ceiling, if you will.
2. A School can provide you insights into your blind spots. Only in the frictions of interacting will you begin to Learn where you really need to do Self-work.

Q. Isn't the LHP just Satanism?
A. If you mean does the LHP postulate a Cosmos run by a good guy and a bad guy, and that we're on the side of the bad guy— no, we are emphatically not Satanists. If you see a Cosmos run by regular laws, which is opposed by desire, and you use "Satan" as a emblem of that desire, then we are Satanists. The archetype of the rebel against cosmic injustice is a powerful one for many people beginning the LHP; such a Model can help the Initiate burn off guilt and complexes and free him- or herself of the debris of past belief systems. But such a Model will not sustain one very long— to simply oppose what Is, is to be chained to it. In the dimmest levels of our society now, there is great opposition to what Is; this is understandable as part of the process of historical change. Unfortunately that has made Satan into a very commercial symbol that can sell clothes, magazines, and music. For the serious LHP practitioner, Satan became powerless when he became cool.

Q. Is Magic really Necessary to Initiation?
A. Yes. It is needed for four distinct reasons.
1. It provides a deep sense of wonder at one's possibilities. As we know, magic in this world is usually worked through prayer, which involves focusing the Will on a collective focus of mankind's consciousness, which is seen as powerful enough to do the deed. When it does Work, a sense of faith is generated in the person who said the prayer. (It might bother him that other people pray to different gods and get results, but that sort of

question is usually resolved by bigotry or guilt.) The magician Learns that he or she is something more than what the world says they are. That creates a type of Knowledge that anchors them in their quest.

2. As the magician begins to develop a lifestyle that will let him or her achieve happiness, the platform from which he or she works will have to be as unique as the reward he/she seeks— to Create a unique platform in this world, you need hard work, intelligent planning, self knowledge, and magic.

3. Magic works best when the Self is unified. This gives the magician a practical reason in the Here-and-Now to unify the Self, rather than hoping that somehow all the Work he/she is doing will payoff in the afterlife.

4. Magic transcends the intellect. Most people that encounter a belief system other than the one they were raised in, merely read about it and think they understand. Initiation isn't about reading, it is about Doing. If the expectation of magical activity is not held forth, people will merely collect books thinking somehow they are better for the amount of dead trees they have in their home.

Q. You prattle on a great deal about ethics— isn't that just to get the media off your back? Can't the true Lord of the Left Hand Path do anything he or she wants?

A. The true initiate can work really hard for nineteen years and maybe you'll be a Lord. The LHP initiate is seeking immortality. If they allow themselves to be a jerk, they are setting up to be a jerk for all time. Jerks are fairly stupid, they don't have much flexibility of perception, they can't appreciate subtle things, they have few true friends. It takes no training to be a jerk, there is no pride of accomplishment in one's jerk-hood. Let the ways of the brutes belong to the brutes, and those of philosopher kings belong to philosopher kings. Now, sadly, there are jerks that hang their shingles out as LHP gurus. They are no different than those people who write self help books on how to bully people. Have fun with them.

Q. What is your model of the afterlife? I want some kind of proof that what you're saying is so— or is this just another goddamn religion?

A. I would love some objective proof (as opposed to subjective or philosophical proofs) as well. If anyone is on the LHP out of faith in my (or other people's) model of the afterlife, then they are in just another goddamn religion. The only thing that a member of a LHP should be able to say with objective certainty on their death bed is "I wouldn't have done anything differently. I have no regrets." My model of the afterlife is that it is possible to build a permanent independent consciousness that interacts with the material universe as desired, by hard work during this life.

Q. Aren't you simply being arrogant when you say that you don't want unity with the universe? Isn't everyone simply part of the All?

A. If an acorn falls from a great oak, it contains all the necessary potentials to be a great oak. But the acorn's job isn't to rot so that it can be absorbed by the root system of the oak. It doesn't seek unity. Instead it seeks to become another oak, which in its own time will make its own acorns. Love does not consist in my being one with the soul of my Lover, but contemplating all the things that make her special and unique from me and from the rest of the Cosmos. If I were at one with her, the amount of Love in our private world would be halved. With each new soul that claims for itself the heritage of the Prince of Darkness, the amount of Love, Mystery, Intelligence, Magic, Play, Music, Memory, Beauty, and Victory all increase in the Cosmos — in fact it is **only** through self development of individual men and women that such Qualities can increase. To desire unity with the universe would be to turn your back on being part of such Work. It may be fine for the weak, but not for us: the adventure is too strong, the goals too worthy.

Of course, most acorns do not grow into oaks. Some rot and feed the daddy oak, others are eaten by squirrels or insects, others simply harden. This is the way of the cosmic ecology. It is the process whereby the Black Order, seeking only its self-preservation, creates the whole of human history, psychology, and civilization. In this frankly painful process, the Black Order was, is, and shall be the mainspring for all that is worthwhile in human life. Blessed be the Black Order!

Some Books, Films, and Tapes
These resources are of a fourfold nature. Firstly they are very useful books, films, and tapes. Secondly they give your sorcery something to Work on. You will learn that sorcery is a combination of projecting a desire, forgetting about that desire so that it can work in the world rather than in your head, and then watching for opportunities to find the books. Thirdly they show the types of things that can be used by a Left Hand Path Initiate— notice how they are not all occult books, and how they come from very different parts of life. Fourthly trying to get these books you will have to learn different skills and go to different places than you normally go; this is an example for you of the Quest. In the Quest, your will is fixed on an object which is Unknown to you, and the process of obtaining that object will change you and bring you into contact with new resources and opportunities.

These books are my recommendations. Some of the authors would certainly **not** endorse my ideas, and do not think of their books as aids to the Left Hand Path.

1. *Lords of the Left-Hand Path: A History of Spiritual Dissent,* by Stephen E. Flowers. Smithville: Rûna-Raven Press (POB 557, Smithville, Texas 78957), 1997. This is an essential book. It covers the history of both Western and Eastern branches of the Left Hand Path. One can not be an informed practitioner without this book, which can give you a realistic idea of what can be done by a Left Hand Path magician, and historical resources for your magical philosophical Quests. Of all the books on the list, probably the only must-have.

2. *Synchronicity: Science, Myth and the Trickster* by Allan Combs and Mark Holland. New York: Marlowe and Company, 1996. This book examines the underlying principle of magic, which is synchronicity, by

102

looking at its modern students: Jung, Pauli, Krammerer, Arthur Koestler, Werner Heisenberg, and David Bohm; as well as its psychological and mythical antecedents. Magic is the art of communicating with the Hidden side of the universe, and learning to read the responses to your signals is one of the first steps in Initiation.

3. *The Psychology of Man's Possible Evolution* by Peter D. Ouspensky. New York: Alfred A. Knopf, 1969. This book, although flawed by its overinsistence on intellectual development, explains in a series of lectures the nature of self-work and the Need for a School. (If you should catch the Gurdjieff bug, follow up with Ouspensky's *In Search of the Miraculous*, New York: Harcourt, Brace & World, 1949.)

4. *Flow: the Psychology of Optimal Experience* by Mihaly Csikszentmihalyi. New York: Harper & Row, 1990. This book explains the psychological goal of life as mindful and pleasurable challenge. This book better describes the emotional state a traveler on the Left Hand Path should have than any number of occult tomes. After #1, the most essential book in this list.

5. *The Stars My Destination* by Alfred Bester (various editions beginning 1956). This science fiction thriller is a great book about Initiation. It shows how magical Secrets are discovered in times of need, how the Initiate has a hard but interesting life, the importance of adventure, the need for versatility, and the Teaching method of the Left Hand Path— putting power in the hands of many diverse folk who are motivated. All of this in a great prose style and tons of action!

6. *The Key to it All* by David Allen Hulse. St. Paul: Llewellyn, 1993 (two volumes). This massive tome will introduce you to a variety of magical Symbol systems. It will help make you aware of what goes into a cosmology, how symbols work on both magicians and the cultures they live in, and how symbol systems may be used for divination. There is a good deal of occult history in these volumes. *Book One* deals with Cuneiform, Hebrew, Arabic, Sanskrit, Tibetan, and Chinese. *Book Two* deals with Greek, Coptic, Runes, Latin, Enochian, Tarot, and English. This is a great launching point for other studies.

7. *An Introduction to Hermetics* by Franz Bardon. Wuppertal: Rüggeberg, 1971. This book is a valuable example of what magical training should be. The author has a practical approach to learning, and is frank about the level of hard skills needed. The translation lacks quality, but until I've written *Uncle Setnakt's One-Year Magical Boot Camp* it is (sadly) the best book I know of in English.

8. *Rites and Symbols of Initiation* by Mircea Eliade (tr. W. Trask) New York: Harper and Row, 1958 (also published as *Birth and Rebirth*). Eliade's works are generally recommended for LHP magicians, but this study of initiatory process in all sorts of societies is a great foundation for understanding what one is trying to do along the Left Hand Path.

9. *The Future of the Body* by Michael Murphy. New York: A Jeremy P. Tarcher/Putnam Book, 1992. This huge tome (787 pages!) is a comprehensive mind-expanding look at body training. Although occasionally drifting too far into the stormy seas of pseudoscience, this

book will tell you more about the types of esoteric body training than anywhere else. Recommended for anyone with a body.

10. *The Age of Analysis: 20th Century Philosophers* by Morton White. Boston: Houghton Mifflin, 1955. This book, also available as a Meridan paperback, is a selection of philosophical texts introduced by Morton White, a Professor at the Institute for Advanced Study in Princeton, N. J. He covers the thoughts, writings, times, and personalities of several twentieth century philosophers. This introduces the Initiate to the vital thoughts of his or her time. Philosophers covered include G. E. Moore, Bertrand Russell, Benedetto Croce, Jean-Paul Sartre, William James, John Dewey, Charles Peirce, George Santayana, Alfred North Whitehead, and Ludwig Wittgenstein. If you wish your Will to Work upon the ideas of your time, you must know the ideas of your time.

11. *Spiral Dynamics* by Don Edward Beck and Christopher C. Cowan. Cambridge: Blackwell Publishers, 1996. This is a complex and realistic book about change process, explaining the refinement of many person systems and single individuals. It is a wonderful text for magicians trying to make their world better. Although the book is entirely secular in its orientation, it is firmly LHP in its view of the world. A good book for people that want to climb the corporate ladder, make a million bucks, and achieve enlightenment.

12. *The Occult in America* edited by Howard Kerr and Charles L. Crow. University of Illinois Press: Chicago and Urbana, 1983. (If you are not living in the U.S.A., you will need to find a similar book for your region.) This sociological and historical survey deals with American occultism, touching on aspects of occult practice, such as class level of occultists and hoaxing, that most occultists are afraid to look at. The LHP Initiate needs to know the weaknesses of the occult world, as well as looking for socioeconomic components of its thinking that he or she may well have absorbed unwittingly. This a good book to bring clarity and balance.

13. *The Art of Worldly Wisdom: A Pocket Oracle* by Baltasar Gracian (translated by Christopher Maurer). New York: Bantam. 1991. This small book written by the Jesuit Baltasar Gracian is a succinct meditation on gaining power, wisdom, dignity, and true Nobility. It is the **best** oracle for day-to-day decisions in the workaday world. Other translations are available but are not as good.

14. *Dealing with the Devil* by William Pridgen. Smithville: Rûna-Raven Press, [forthcoming]. This book deals with late twentieth century manifestations of the Left Hand Path. A good guide to the rise and fall of LHP groups as well as a study of the psychological and historical factors that are making the Left Hand Path appealing. Since the desire for the Path currently outstrips the numbers of Teachers available, only the most dedicated will make headway in real Schools. From the point of view of cosmic ecology this is a good thing; it will Create a band of Elite Teachers in the next few decades, which is part of the Great Working in the world. Unfortunately it also means that many people without a clue will try forming their own schools based on having a webpage and access to a photocopy machine.

15. *5,000 Years with the God Set*. Audio cassette, 85 minutes. Wolfslair, Inc. (8033 Sunset Boulevard #1313, Los Angeles, CA 90046). Don Webb, the High Priest of Set talks at Hellhouse of Hollywood on Set through antiquity to his remanifestation as Symbol for Left Hand Path Initiation. This is a study of the effect of the Prince of Darkness as an idea upon men and women. This talk preceded a global magical Working to Strengthen the Typhonic current in the world.

16. *Call Me the Prince of Darkness*. Video cassette. Wolfslair, Inc. Don Webb, High Priest of Set, is interviewed on current Left Hand Path practices, and on the Temple in particular. Critics of various stripes discuss the idea of the Left Hand Path. This tape provides an experience of seeing a current practitioner, and seeing what critics say about the practice. If you can't afford it, you can practice your metacommunication skills and get the "cool" video rental place in your town to do so.

17. *Meetings with Remarkable Men*. Film, 1979. This British-made film directed by Peter Brook is Gurdjieff's magical autobiography. In stunning and beautiful scenes the nature of the Quest, of the need for Travel, of the need to Synthesize different ideas, of metacommunication ("American Canaries"), training in differing levels of the self, and the importance of art and crafts to Initiation is shown. This is available as a video cassette.

18. *The Occult Experience*. Video cassette, 1990. This made-for-television movie by Neville Drury features interviews with many types of current occultists from Right Hand Path and Left Hand Path groups. Michael and Lilith Aquino are interviewed to represent the Temple of Set, and clips of Anton La Vey in the film *Satanis* are shown. The film shows some of the silliness of the New Age movement as well as making some legitimate observations on mankind's need for a new spirituality.

19. *Rûnarmâl-I: The Rûna Talks* by Stephen Edred Flowers. Smithville, Texas: Rûna-Raven Press, 1991. This is the essential text for persons wishing to learn about Flowers' V° Word of *RUNA*. It is much more universal than Flowers' other books, and explains the relationship between Xeper and Rûna. I consider it one of the most important magical texts working in the world today.

The Temple of Set

The Temple of Set is an international organization existing on every continent except Antarctica, and it is the only Satanic religion fully recognized by the United States government. Its membership is limited to adults (18+) and is open to all races, genders, and gender preferences. Its only requirement of its members is their desire to use the Temple of Set as a tool for their self development.

The Temple of Set is a Left Hand Path Initiatory organization. The tradition of spiritual dissent in the West has been called Satanism, but more universally the Left Hand Path is a rationally intuited spiritual technology for the purpose of self deification. We choose as our role model the ancient Egyptian god Set, the archetype of Isolate Intelligence, rather than the somewhat limiting Hebrew Satan, archetype of Rebel against cosmic injustice. As part of our practice we each seek the

105

deconstruction of the socially constructed mind, so we begin in rebellion— thus we accept the label "Satanist," but since we seek to supplant the socially constructed mind with a mind of our own individually chosen construction, we prefer the term Setian. We have no "religious" interest in the figure of Satan, and indeed we do not worship Set— worshiping instead only our own potential.

As an Initiatory organization we do not provide any services for the profane world. We don't allow the curious to attend our rites, we don't seek affiliation with other religious groups, we don't agree that there is a universal truth behind all religions. Because of our elitist attitude and because of our antinomian attitudes, we have been tarred with a variety of false labels by the more simplistic members of society. We have been accused of crimes, and accused of racism, sexism, and whatever other "isms" contemporary society views as evil. The fact that a moment's effort on the part of a serious journalist dispels these myths has little effect on popular opinion. Such resistance from the forces of stupidity is Initiatorally beneficial, as it provides the need for a certain inner strength. I would like to examine the nature of the Left Hand Path, which will provide some understanding on why it is feared and loathed, an introduction to Set, an explanation of the operations of the Temple of Set, some remarks on urban legends, and provide contact information for persons seriously seeking information about the Temple.

The Left Hand Path as Seen by the Temple of Set
The Temple of Set views mankind as being set apart from other animals. Our existence transcends the mere stimulus-response approach to the pleasures and pains of existence. This quality of Being (as Heidegger has remarked) has always led to the two essential questions of Western philosophy— the grounding question of "Why is there Being rather than Nothingness?" and the guiding question of philosophy "What is the nature of Being?" All schools of inquiry — as opposed to those of faith — have struggled with these questions. For schools not taking a nihilistic path, a third question has evolved, "Given the nature of Being, what actions should be taken?" The last is the question of guiding one's life in accordance with what may be rationally deduced. The Temple's synthesis, while not historically unique, is different from that of most current philosophies.

The Buddha, who is perhaps the purest Right Hand Path philosopher, answered the question of the nature of Being as "Being is suffering." He saw (and rightly so) that Being was furthered by Desire, and that led to a permanence of the Self and greater suffering for the Self. His solution was to eliminate Desire and harmonize the elements of the psyche with those of the objective universe. The Left Hand Path rejects the ethical imperative of this notion. We see "Being is Knowing" and the ethical imperative is to further the permanence of the Self by embracing the pleasures and pains of existence. We exalt and revel in the disharmony our Desire brings; we accept the pains that come from trying to make our dreams come true; we realize that the absolute responsibility for our actions is our own.

106

The conclusion of "Being is Knowing" is reflected by the examination of our lives. If there were no purpose to intelligent existence, the appropriate response would be a hedonistic nihilism— a path favored by many "Satanic" organizations currently. We choose to affirm purpose to existence in part because we are magicians and magic is an ascriptive process, and in part because it is a source of Joy and Strength— always goals for the Left Hand Path. The Temple of Set views life as the process of the psyche coming to know its own existence and then to expand that existence in as many realms as are open to it. We therefore value both power in this world, and the Self-given promise of power in a postmortem state. Seeking to increase one's power and pleasure is therefore a sacred duty. The Temple of Set rejects nihilism— observing (as did Maurice Blanchot) that you can not **use** negation if you dwell within it.

Our Word is an ancient Egyptian verb, "Xeper," pronounced "Kheffer." Written with the hieroglyph of the scarab beetle, it means "I Have Come Into Being." This is a twofold assertion. Firstly it is one of Joy and Self-love, and is a guide to those who can say it with Pride as to what subsequent actions they should take. It is a mandate for self improvement — particularly of transforming life into a series of pleasurable challenges rather then mindless hedonism. The Setian seeks to transform mundane life into a species of Play, by hard work, ambition, and Black Magic (see below). Secondly the word of Xeper is a statement of the only cosmic fact we can possess— a Divine form of Descartes' "Cogito" if you will.

"Xeper" is the Setian's answer to the latter two questions above, but we have to look to the grounding question of philosophy as well, "Why Being rather than Nothingness?" This leads to the perception of the Prince of Darkness. Now such "cosmogonic questions" are useful as attitude adjusters— as providing a sense of wonder, which is necessary for magical action. The Right Hand Path chooses personifications of natural forces as role models to be harmonized with— in the Right Hand Path's more extreme forms the universe as a whole is personified as God or the Will of God. The Setian chooses as role model a "god against the gods." We choose an archetype that corresponds with the disharmonizing part of our own psyches. We look for a role model that seeks its own extension and self-knowledge through action. This role model is the "Lord of this World," who is rejected by the Right Hand Path as the Prince of Darkness. The Urge to expand Being is exemplified by Set, whose enemies are Death/Stasis (Osiris) and Delusion of Unity with the Cosmos (Apep). Set was and is the patron of the magician who seeks to increase his existence though expansion. Set's motives are the answer to the grounding question of philosophy "Why Being rather than Nothingness?" We see Set's magical action in us in the same light that we see our magical action on the world. We refer to this as the Gift of Set, an Egyptian phrase for the wine produced in the Oasis of Kharga— where boiling sulfur springs fed the vines that made the sweetest wine in ancient Egypt. Thus we make of our Desire our immortal selves.

One of our senior Initiates penned a good description of Set and his Gift:

I.   Set is the Principle of Isolate Intelligence.
II. It is dynamic (evolving).
III. Its purpose is self-maintenance, expansion, and perpetuation. This is its only good— otherwise it is beyond good and evil.
IV. It is not omnipotent— it must work for the changes it causes.
V.   It is not omniscient— it must work to see objectively.
VI. Its Gift of Self is *perfect* (complete).
VII. It can *inform* or "teach" those possessed of its quality.
VIII. To give more (if possible) would be to *take*.
IX. The presence of the Gift in us (flesh) is *necessary* to the evolution of the Principle of Isolate Intelligence.

We see Satanism not so much as getting humanity to accept a guy with a pair of horns but to accept their own (Forgotten) better natures; and the method that lets people find this Remembering is through antinomianism — not merely rejecting the spiritual traditions of society, but critically rejecting most of society's programming methods from advertising to superstition. The mission of the Temple of Set is to recreate a Tradition of self-deification that was once respected by the wise, as can be seen in Plato's *Symposium*.

I would like to look at the historical ways that Set has been perceived, but I must emphasize that the Temple is not a "neo-Egyptian religion." Although we give Egypt a special place in our studies, we search out all aspects of the archetype of the Prince of Darkness— both traditional and those of our own making.

SET

The oldest known form of the Prince of Darkness, the archetype of Isolate Intelligence, is the Egyptian god Set, whose Priesthood can be traced to predynastic times. Images of Set have been dated to ca. 3200 BCE, with astronomically-based estimates of inscriptions dating to 5000 BCE. Set's name originally meant "cutter" or "isolator"— he is a personification of the process of Initiation — of Becoming more and more your own self. Setians do not pray to Set, nor does he care about their day-to-day lives. Setians emulate Set, and further the process of individuation and Initiation on this world. Set is a complex figure, a much better role model than the limited figure of the Judeo-Christian Satan. Satan, the archetype of the rebel against cosmic injustice, may be where many people begin the lifelong process of Initiation, but he is too small a symbol for the richness of the Left Hand Path.

The Egyptian god Set went through periods of immense popularity alternating with total denunciation. Set in the predynastic and archaic periods was an essentially positive deity introduced from the east as a god of the *extension of existence*. He is therefore god of *expanding* borders and radical changes of being, particularly birth, circumcision/initiation, death in battle, and rebirth through the Opening of the Mouth ceremony. Popular among easterners, his first cult site being Pelusium in the eastern Delta, Set's worship quickly spread to *border* areas, where he was identified with local gods of initiation. Two examples of such cult sites are Kharga in the south, which has always been primarily a Nilotic culture area, and the Libyan settlement of Ombos, wherein Set was identified with the local god Ash in the IInd dynasty. Set's original worship as a nighttime/polar deity suffered a decline with the rise of solar worship in the IVth dynasty. The Great Pyramid of Khufu is one of the last early monuments connected with the idea of a Setian afterlife as well as a solar one. The Great Pyramid had a special air shaft for the king's *akh* to fly to the stars of Set.

During the Middle Kingdom, Set was reduced to a symbol of Upper Egypt and apparently seen only during the Setian festival of *heb-sed*, or tying together. It was during this time that Set was first blamed for the murder of Osiris, a Semitic corn god who had arrived in the IIIrd dynasty. Previously, Osiris had died of drowning. No matter how "evil" Set was, the essential function of Set, of going out and expanding the borders of existence and then returning that Chaotic energy to the center, always continued. It is the darkness that binds together the Egyptian light. The murder of Osiris is the destruction of the fetters of society, of accepting self-change and cultivation over the forces that lead to self stagnation.

The foreigners who ruled Egypt who were known as the Hyksos, actively identified themselves with Set and established their capital at an ancient Setian site, Avaris. Very little is known about their religious or magical practices, although excavations going on at the time of this writing should reveal great wealth. But they were great horsemen, and the horse had became identified with Set. It required Hyksos rule before, after almost 200 years of its use in Egypt, that evil Setian animal the horse could be portrayed in Egyptian art.

The second native blooming of Setian thinking may have begun in the XVIIIth dynasty, but certainly it reached its peak in the XIXth and XXth dynasties when a family of Setian priests from Tanis became the pharaonic line. During this time of expanding borders, Set was extraordinarily popular, as can be seen from pharaohs' names such as Seti (= Set's man) and Setnakt (= Set is Mighty). Two important Setian texts were produced: First, the *Tale of Two Brothers* tells how Set (identified with the god Bata, whose name means "Lord of this World") undergoes a series of metamorphoses (Xeperu) that change him from a farm hand to a star in the Constellation of the Thigh. Thus Set is our role model as a man who through his own hard work, magical skill, and the **use** of the resistance of the world— Became divine. The second text is the *Book of Knowing the Spiral Force of Re and the Felling of Apep.* This protective formula, which Ramses III, son of Setnakt, inscribed on certain border monuments, shows two Setian particularities. Firstly, it narrates (from a first person perspective) how an unnamed god comes into being in the psychic (subjective) realm as the god Xephra. Secondly, the spell gives the magician one of the powers of Set, which is to slay Apep, the dragon of delusion. Set likewise serves as a role model, in that each Setian seeks to end delusions in his of her life.

With the coming of the XXIInd dynasty, Egypt entered its long decline. Set became a tremendously unpopular deity. His worship ceased everywhere except the oases and the city of Thebes, where his cult was absorbed into the cult of Montu, the warlord of Thebes. The negative and destructive aspects of isolation and destruction were emphasized and as Egypt turned more to an idealized past, Set-Heh, the god of the void called the future, came to resemble the Christian Satan. The third blooming came with the coming of the Greeks to Egypt. It is from this period that the Hellenic notions of independence and self-worth began to revive both the operant and initiatory aspects of the New Kingdom Set cult. The success of Graeco-Egyptian magic, despite Roman persecution, saw an expansion of both the philosophical and magical aspects of this tradition as far north as Britain. The Third Century of the Common Era was the height of Setian Hermeticism. With the coming of Christianity as a state religion, individualism was again despised. The Coptic fathers identified Set with Satan, and Set almost disappears as a figure in Egyptian magic.

The fourth blooming of Setian thought began in the nineteenth century with certain archaeological discoveries, but it reached a visible stage in 1975 CE when Michael Aquino invoked the Prince of Darkness to seek his advice. On North Solstice 1975 the Prince of Darkness revealed himself to Michael Aquino as Set, and gave us the Word of our Aeon **Xeper**. Michael Aquino and most of the Priesthood of the Church of Satan founded the Temple of Set, and he served as the first of its three High Priests.

The Setian Method

The fight against delusion, against the false beliefs in the world, is a primary Setian occupation. Our three principal methods are Socratic reductionism, the formulation of correct understandings by logic, and noetic intuition. I will examine each of these techniques.

Socratic reductionism. The act of questioning and testing beliefs to eliminate falsehoods is an important tool for arriving at the truth. As we mature all of us ask ourselves, "What beliefs are mine and which have society programmed into me?" Setians, in particular, seek to distance themselves from the vast roar of cultural propaganda. Whereas some groups break from society by merely picking a different prepackaged belief system, the Setian is left with the tough day-to-day struggle of self knowledge and moral relativism. Eventually we each have to become philosophers rather than consumers.

Formulations of correct understandings by logic. Having discarded the untrue and the nonessential, we are left with the building blocks for creating a model of the universe. These notions may have been gained from science, personal experience, from other philosophical/psychological belief systems, or from findings of other Initiates with whom we've chosen to Work. Creative synthesis of ideas — a self-managed dialectic, if you will — has been a major source of human knowledge. Setians begin a creation of a model of the universe in order to understand it (and when necessary, exert control of it through magic and other means). One of the aims of Xeper is to understand the relationship of yourself to the universe. Again this is a tough road. We are placed in the position of Socrates, the wisest man of Greece, who said, "I know nothing." We look upon the universe as an exciting place to study rather than as a dull and finished product.

Noetic inspiration. The third technique, noetic inspiration, takes you to the discovery of your own divinity and the edge of Black Magic. We take the term *noesis* from Plato. Plato defined three types of knowing. The lowest is *pistis* (faith). This means believing something because someone in authority tells you so. The Pope tells you that birth control is wrong, so you know it's wrong. Society is controlled by this level. The next higher way of knowing is *dianoia* (reasoning). This is the test of reason and logic referred to above. The elites work in this level. The highest knowing is *noesis*— direct knowledge. This is the knowing that comes from the divine Self. Examples of it may be found in your personal life— when you've come up with a solution to a problem that was wholly new or novel to you. Or you may have written poetry or music. This flash of inspiration is your psyche becoming aware of its own existence. You may have recognized this sacred quality in something you've seen — the buildings of Gaudi, or reading *Ulysses*, or any of a thousand things. When you encountered this thing and knew, "This is something special. This isn't the product of a meat machine!" then you have experienced this sense. The Temple of Set attempts to create an environment where these experiences may be consciously sought and entered into again and again. Also, I should note, the Temple is only interested in genuine experiences (brought about by Will)— drug users are not welcome and solipsists may take a hike!

Black Magic and Antinomianism

Initiation begins with the denial and rejection of the herd. The cultural and social values of the masses, whether propounded by conventional religions or by mass media, are seen as obstacles to the spiritual development of the individual. Human society values **stasis** above all things. The Initiate seeks positive self change above all things. This means a break with society's values in order to discover one's own is the first step. This is spiritual dissent. In a Judeo-Christian society this is called Satanism. But the Initiate is rebelling against more than the idea of an external "god"; the break is made from external controlling forces of advertising, custom, and superstition as well. To work magic that changes the self, the magician's will must as strong in his or her subjective universe as the massed wills of others appear to be. Once this strength of will is obtained, magical control of life follows. As long as an individual is more strongly motivated by shame or fear or the desire for acceptance, he or she cannot practice magic of an initiatory nature. White magic is the process of calling on personifications of the objective universe to adjust your relation to it in a harmonious way. Most White Magic is a form of prayer. Black Magic is based on self-intuited goals— its formula is "My will be done" as opposed to the White Magic of the Right Hand Path whose formula is "Thy will be done." Black Magic is shunned and feared because to do Black Magic is to take full responsibility for one's actions, evolution, and effectiveness. Now since magic enables the Setian to influence or change events in ways not understood nor anticipated by society, before the Setian puts it to use he or she must first develop a sound and sophisticated appreciation for the ethics governing his or her own motives, decisions, and actions. Merely using magic for impulsive, trivial, or egoistic desires is not Setian. It must become second-nature to the Setian to carefully pre-evaluate the consequences of what he or she wishes to do— then choose the course of wisdom, justice, and creative improvement. It is important to realize that the Temple of Set utilizes a *wide* spectrum of magical tools, far beyond just the "Egyptian," and is always seeking new methods.

Magic may either be operant — spells to cure your mother's illness, get a better job, strengthen your memory — or illustrative/initiatory. The former is the Art of getting what you Need, perhaps the most important Tool in the Setian toolbox. The latter magical formulae deal with enacting the lifetime process of Initiation. They are like the rites of passage performed by religionists, but they are separated from these by an important factor— they represent an individual rather than a social change. Initiatory rites of passage represent the actualization of self-deification. Social rites of passage inform and integrate an individual into society. For example, a rite communicating passage into adulthood informs the society that the individual involved is now possessed of certain responsibilities and powers. An initiatory rite informs the *psyche* of the individual that he or she is now possessed of certain powers and responsibilities. Initiatory magic — when practiced by the individual — separates him- or herself from the social matrix.

Initiation does not occur *within* the magical chamber, but it is illustrated there. One does not enter into adulthood by (say) receiving one's high school diploma, but that action illustrates a variety of other processes which may have occurred. It's easy for the high school graduate to know that *something* has happened, the ritual being boosted by not only his cap and gown, but those of his peers, the music, the crowds, etc. The magician has ultimately only his or her will to provide the knowledge of the change. Magic is the way that the follower of the Left Hand Path can have the **lived experience** of being a god, rather than praying to an image of a god created by his or her imagination.

The best candidate for the Temple of Set will have already have some success with his or her sorcery. Magical ability is a gift; it can not be conferred by any institution. Most of the occultnik world profits from people without magical ability to whom they sell an endless array of books and tools. This regrettable practice weakens the image of the magician and contributes to the dying off of empiricism in our society. Magic, despite what you may have heard, is very hard work. I will discuss the path of an Initiate through the Temple of Set, and then its current structure.

112

Path of an Initiate

Veronica encounters the name of the Temple, and she decides to find out about it. The notion of Xeper, of Willed conscious evolution, appeals to her. Maybe she read about the Order of the Vampyre in Noreen Dresser's *American Vampires* or the article on Satanism in the *Encyclopedia of American Religions.* She writes the San Francisco P. O. box and gets a long informational letter (or visits our webpage). This initial action is one of Magical Curiosity, which is itself soul-transforming. The urge to make the Unknown Known is a preliminary to Xeper. After weeks of weighing the pros and cons — "They seem nice and intelligent, but what's really going on?" — she decides to apply, sending a letter expressing her desire to honestly quest and $65 for materials. After a couple of months of waiting, she is contacted by a member of the Priesthood for an extensive phone interview. Later, she meets the member of the Priesthood at a local coffee house for a period of mutual questioning. Assuming that she makes a good case for her interest (and that she expresses no criminal nor unethical intent), she is admitted. She receives a document called *The Crystal Tablet of Set* and a white medallion, indicating that she is a Setian I°. For her this symbolizes the boldness of the quest for self divinity. For those who will be fortunate enough to Work with her, it symbolizes the excitement and energy of an as-yet-unarticulated Desire— one of the driving forces arising from the Black Flame of self awareness. She's also told that she has two years to bring forth certain qualities in herself, and that she'll need to find a member of the Priesthood to Recognize those qualities within her. Not bestow something on her, not give her an exam to pass, but Recognize. She's scared, intrigued, and challenged. This isn't like any other religion she's been associated with. She's also told that such a Recognition will not take place during her first year of membership. Also, there's this book with chapters named "Black Magic." And a huge reading list, none of it required, on topics that may be of interest to her as she applies the techniques. Some of the topics of interest were what she expected in a Black Magical group, such as Lycanthropy or H. P. Lovecraft. But she wonders how a book on photography, *The Command to Look,* or one on optimal psychology, *Flow,* or on politics, *Political Ideas and Ideologies,* fit into these concepts of magic and religion. She is fortunate that she lives in a town with a Pylon; some towns don't have one yet. The interaction of Initiates of different levels of experience is a source of both challenge and support, so she seeks membership. She meets with the Priest running the Pylon, buys a black robe, and goes to the first meeting, which is a free-form discussion of the application of Setian philosophy to mundane life. The Pylon members like her, she likes them, and she joins. She comes to monthly rituals. At first it's pretty overwhelming. Each member writes Work to satisfy their own personal and emotional needs. Sometimes the Work derives completely from their own formulas— sometimes they adapt historic models. Soon she is trying Work on her own— rituals for destruction, compassion, lust, understanding. Eventually she tries her hand at group Work. She reads the bimonthly newsletter, *The Scroll of Set,* and she starts to correspond with other Setians.

After sixteen months the Priest comes to see in her an understanding of Left-Hand Path philosophy, genuine magical ability (her objective magic Works— she gets the boyfriends and raises she wants), and a commitment to the organization. The Priest Recognizes her as Adept and presents her with a red medallion— confirming that (rather than conferring) her state of Being has passed from Death to Life. At this point she has shown to others and to herself that she can Awaken, See, and Act — which Setians view as the highest human achievement. She will likely stay an Adept for the rest of her life — since that is the level with the least formal obligation to the Temple. Adepts are graduates of the system, rather than teachers, and it is in the mode of Adept that all of us interact with the world.

The year of her Recognition, she decides to go to the annual International Conclave. She gets to meet Setians from Australia, Germany, the United Kingdom, Finland, etc. The magical and social interaction of Conclave accelerated her progress immensely. She's planning to go next year— saving up her money since it will be in Europe.

As an Adept, she has mastered the basic concepts of the Temple. She is free now to specialize— rather like the completion of her basic college courses. She may choose to affiliate with an Order of the Temple— a group led by a Fourth Degree, a Magister Templi. The Work of Orders is mainly confidential, but if you're interested you may wish to read about the *Order of the Vampyre* in Noreen Dresser's American Vampires, or purchase Stephen Edred Flowers' *Black Rûna,* which concerns the Order of the Trapezoid.

Veronica may consciously seek the next level of Initiation. The Third Degree — that of Priest or Priestess of Set — is characterized by responsibility and divinity. Here the Initiate seeks the touch of Set himself. This is not a unification with Set, but an alignment with the force that gave mankind awareness. For those that achieve this goal, there is a considerable strengthening of the Will. It is a position not without strain— for those necessary controls to a strong Will, patience and wisdom, must be cultivated by the individual. The three Initiatory Degrees beyond Priest — Magister, Magus, and Ipsissimus — may be thought of as further refinements of this initial alignment. There is a great deal more to these, but that is discovered better through personal interaction than through words. The key to understanding the degree system is the word *Recognition.* There are no special honors that come with various colored medallions. No bowing and scraping. An Initiate can correspond with/interact with anyone that finds that interaction beneficial. Since our religion is tuned toward personal growth, it becomes important to stress different stages of growth. This gives the individual outward examples to test their growth against, and keeps them from sinking into a mire of subjectivity. In some organizations titles are sold (or given away through simple seniority). If you start out as Grand Exalted Pooh-Bah, there is no place to go. The Temple provides a wonderful toolkit. You can see real growth both inside and outside of yourself. The Temple is a training ground for Work in the wide world. It is a tool, not an alternative universe.

The Temple's Structure
The following two sections are drawn largely from the Temple's General Information Letter.

The deliberately individualistic atmosphere of the Temple of Set is not easily conducive to group activities on a routine or programmed basis. There are no congregations of docile "followers"— only cooperative philosophers and magicians.

Executive authority in the Temple is held by the Council of Nine, which appoints both the High Priest of Set and the Executive Director. Initiates are Recognized according to six degrees: Setian I°, Adept II°, Priest or Priestess of Set III°, Magister/Magistra Templi IV°, Magus/Maga V°, and Ipsissimus/Ipsissima VI°.

The design, care, and operation of the Temple are entrusted by Set to the Priesthood. All Initiates of the Priesthood are originally highly-qualified Adepts in the Black Arts. Most of your contact with them will be in this context. Because they are responsible for the integrity of the Temple as a whole, however, they have the authority both to evaluate and Recognize Initiates' competence and, if necessary, to suspend or expel individuals who have proven themselves incapable of maintaining Setian standards of dignity and excellence. The Priesthood takes all of these responsibilities extremely seriously, since it regards its name literally and its trust as sacred. In this respect it stands significantly apart from conventional religious clergy, who *de facto* consider their "priesthoods" as social professions and their deities as mere symbols and metaphors for their institutional or personal exploitation.

The knowledge of the Temple of Set is made available through four principal avenues: an extensive (and ever-expanding) reading list of published works in twenty-four specialized fields; the newsletter *Scroll of Set*; the publications of the Temple's various specialized Orders; and the series of encyclopedias entitled the *Jeweled Tablets of Set*. The contents of the *Scroll* and the Order periodicals are time-dated, of course, but those of the *Tablets* change periodically as ideas are advanced, improved, or disproved; or as they become more or less relevant to the Temple's areas of concern. The *Scroll*, Order newsletters, and *Tablets* are reproduced simply and inexpensively to preclude excessive membership expenditure for frequently-revised publications.

Many Initiates are geographically distant from one another. This necessitates an organizational design geared more towards services to the individual than to localized "congregations." Recognizing the value — and fellowship — of a seminar environment, however, the Temple provides for "Pylons" (named after the unique gates of ancient Egyptian temples). Pylons are often geographically localized, but some are "correspondence" Pylons with global membership and interaction. While each Pylon is under the trust and responsibility of a II°+ Sentinel, they are emphatically not "leader/follower congregations," but rather cooperative and interactive forums for individual Initiates. Each new Setian is expected to affiliate with at least one Pylon within a year of admission to the Temple and Recognition to the II° will normally be recommended and/or formalized by that Pylon. Recognitions to the II° generally occur after the first year of membership.

Individuals admitted to the Temple are provided with a personal copy of the *Crystal Tablet of Set*, which contains a wide range of organizational, philosophical, and magical information pertinent to qualification as an Adept. There is a two-year time-limit for each new Setian to qualify for Adept Recognition. If such Recognition is not received by that time, affiliation is canceled.

The Orders of the Temple are entirely different in concept and operation from its Pylons. Each Order specializes in one or more particular field of the magical arts and sciences. Such a specialization may be transcultural or oriented to a specific geographic area, time-period, or conceptual tradition. Within one year after II° Recognition, each Adept is expected to affiliate with an Order resonate with his or her personal interests and aptitudes. The collective knowledge of all of the Orders is available to the Temple membership generally.

Setians are encouraged to communicate with one another by means of a regularly-updated InterCommunication Roster (contained in the *Crystal Tablet*), and periodic Conclaves and gatherings are scheduled on a regional, national, and international basis.

Personal affiliation with the Temple is kept confidential; a Setian's admission is known only to the Priesthood.

Since the Temple considers other religions as inherently false, membership in other religious bodies is not permitted beyond the I°. Setians may pursue membership in other Initiatory Orders. The Temple does not seek however to undermine or attack other religions, we view them as purveyors of socially useful myths that provide ethical standards for persons unable to think on their own. We do however recognize the need for free speech and practice and Setians are encouraged to be active on these fronts— even defending the rights of those hostile to us.

Urban Folklore

It is regrettable that a simplistic view of Satanism drawn from movies, Christian propaganda, and superstition has led to an urban myth of Satanists as "baby-eating, blood-drinking fiends." This type of folklore, which is as realistic as stories of microwaved poodles or the Alaskan "mute-rat," have long since been discredited by serious studies by the FBI and British law enforcement officials. Unfortunately these stories are still passed around as an urban legend of Satanism — sometimes broadened to include all occultists— sometimes sadly passed by occultists wanting to provide a scapegoat to an uneasy crowd (It's THEM not US). The fact of the matter is that we have not found that any interest or activity which an enlightened, mature intellect would regard as undignified, criminal, or depraved is desirable, much less essential to our work.

The Temple of Set is an evolutionary product of human experience. Such experience includes the magical and philosophical work of many occult individuals and organizations which have preceded us. Some of these were socially acceptable by contemporary or modern standards; others were not. Some made brilliant discoveries in one field of interest while blighting their reputations with shocking excesses or tragic failures in others. In examining the secret and suppressed corners of history for valuable and useful material, the Temple insists upon ethical presentation and use of such discoveries as it makes. Setians who are in any doubt as to the ethics involved in any of the fields which we explore are expected to seek counsel from the Priesthood. All Setians are further expected to display a high measure of maturity and common sense in this area.

The Black Arts are **dangerous** in the same way that working with volatile chemicals is dangerous. This is most emphatically **not** a field for unstable, immature, or otherwise emotionally or intellectually weak-minded people. Such are a hazard to themselves and to others with whom they come into contact. The Temple endeavors to not admit them to begin with. If such an individual should gain admittance and later be exposed, he or she will be summarily expelled. In cases of doubt the Temple may be expected to place the burden of proof on the individual, for the sake of all Setians and the Temple's integrity. If you desire more information on the Temple of Set, the General Information Letter is available from:

Temple of Set
Post Office Box 470307
San Francisco, CA 94147

or you visit our website:
http://www.xeper.org
Xepera Xeper Xeperu

"I Have Come Into Being,
and by the Process of my Coming Into Being,
the Process of Coming Into Being is Established."

Uncle Setnakt Says Farewell to his Readers

To those collectors of occult books who have made sure that this tiny book is passed on by your estate, I send you my thanks in helping me Send my message to the future!

To those angry people who destroyed this book, rather than recycled it at a used book store, I send my wish that your resources are wasted as you do Mother Earth's.

To those who read the book with an open mind, but honestly decided you disagree with my message, I send my respect. May your life be blessed with thoughtful people such as yourself.

To those of you who found the book too hard going, since it is written at a college level, I send my recommendations to look into some further education because you'll need it, on any Path you choose.

To those of you who read the entire book with the hairy eyeball, because you promised a loved one you would, I send my fullest admiration. Regardless of our differences, we agree that it is important to do things for love.

To those of you that disregarded the book, but tried reading the rituals aloud as spells, I send my contempt. Magic is not for the careless; fortunately your lack of talent stopped everything anyway.

To those of you who read the book, tried out the suggestions, and came to the conclusion that the Left Hand Path was not for you, I send my regard. Brave people such as yourself make the world a better place to live in.

To those of you who read the book in preparation of writing a few dismissive lines on the Left Hand Path, which you had planned to write anyway, I send similar prejudice into the world to work against you on a personal level.

To those of you who read the book, and have put its very difficult recommendations into practice, I Send the news that you will go far, and if your Purpose does not fail, you will become a Lord or Lady of the Left Hand Path. To such as these, Uncle Setnakt sends his Blessings and his Love!

4/3/XXXIII AES

H E S L O T D
T T E V O L L
L B C O R I V
1 1 8

Rûna-Raven Titles of Related Interest

Black Rûna   Stephen Edred Flowers
This contains articles written for *Runes,* the journal of the Order of the Trapezoid, which have been found to be of general interest. This work will go a long way toward demonstrating the character of symbolic and magical work within the Order, and will fill in some "gaps" in the public's knowledge concerning the works of Edred Thorsson. This strictly limited collectors edition reveals for the first time some of the inner documents of the Order of the Trapezoid. The Introduction includes biographical data and material from the *Lords of the Left-Hand Path* manuscript.

(Edition limited to 504 copies) $31.00

Carnal Alchemy: A *Sado-Magical Exploration of Pleasure, Pain and Self-Transformation*   Crystal Dawn and Stephen Flowers
This text re-introduces a powerful philosophy and magical technology to the contemporary world of western sexual magic. Sadomasochistic sexuality is among the least understood aspects of sexual expression. It is tinged with overtones of the mysterious and forbidden — these things, as well as physiological facts about it — make it a powerful form of sexuality to be combined with spiritual or magical aims.

$13.00

Lords of the Left-Hand Path   Stephen E. Flowers
This is a huge compendium study of Left-Hand Path individuals and groups from ancient times to modern movements such as the Church of Satan and the Temple of Set— both of which have indi-vidual chapters in the book. Ancient paths include the Egyptian cult of Set, Hinduism, Buddhism, Zoroastrianism, the Yezidis, Neoplatonists and the Greeks, the Germanics, the Slavs, the Assass-ins, Dualist sects, the Faustian path, the Hellfire Club, de Sade, Marx and the sinister aspects of Bolshevism. A chapter is devoted to Hitler and Himmler and "Nazi occultism." Other individuals analyzed include Blavatsky, Gurdjieff, Crowley, Spare, Gregorius and Gerald Gardner.

$36.00

The New Flesh Palladium   Robert North
The long-awaited manifesto of the New Flesh Palladium, a sex-magical order headed by Robert North, the translator of Paschal Beverly Randolph's infamous *Sexual Magic.* The author traces the development of the idea of the New Flesh through the intellectual worlds of the 17th through 20th centuries— exploring the ideas of Swedenborg, Sade, Thomas Lake Harris, Randolph, Crowley, Spare and Wilhelm Reich.

$16.00

Rúnarmál I   Stephen Edred Flowers

The title means "Sayings of the Rune." This is a compilation of 11 essays based on a series of talks given by Edred over the course of the spring and summer of 1991ev. Their intent was to explore the concept underlying the Runes— *Rûna*. As such the work is a study in the operative formula hidden within the present Runic stream. Most of the contents of these essays have, until now, only been available as oral teachings. This is the most significant work to appear in years in the Runic Tradition— and provides a key to other works.

$13.00

The Seven Faces of Darkness: Practical Typhonian Magic Don Webb

Here is a book which penetrates to the core of the Typhonian current active in the world today— and does so by returning to the very fountain-heads of Setian practice and philosophy. Never before has anyone made the true Typhonian current more plain and objective, in practice or in theory.

$16.00

To order these or any other Rûna-Raven titles, write to:

Rûna-Raven
Post Office Box 557
Smithville, Texas 78957
U.S.A.

Include $3.00 postage for first item, and $1.00 for each additional item.

120